E

Also in the LONG RIDER *series*

LONG RIDER

KILLER MUSTANG

CLAY DAWSON

12

CHARTER/DIAMOND BOOKS, NEW YORK

KILLER MUSTANG

A Charter/Diamond Book/published by arrangement with
the author

PRINTING HISTORY
Charter/Diamond edition/September 1990

ISBN: 1-55773-389-9

Charter/Diamond Books are published by The Berkley Publishing
Group, 200 Madison Avenue, New York, New York 10016.
The name "CHARTER/DIAMOND" and its logo are trademarks
belonging to Charter Communications, Inc.

PRINTED IN THE UNITED STATES OF AMERICA

10 9 8 7 6 5 4 3 2 1

CHAPTER ONE

Long Rider raised himself up in his stirrups and let his powerful sorrel gelding blow clouds of steam into the frigid Utah air. Barely visible to the southwest was the great Salt Lake, and in every other direction there were vast stretches of sage leading toward distant, hazy blue mountains. It was an immense country, harshly beautiful and untamed. In Ogden and Salt Lake City the industrious Mormons under Brigham Young had turned desert into oasis, but they would not do that in this rough, rocky country. This land was good for nothing except cattle and mustangs.

Long Rider turned in his stirrups, his gray eyes missing nothing around him. And even though his sorrel was an exceptionally large and powerful animal, Long Rider seemed too big for the horse. In fact, he stood six foot two, which was tall, but not exactly the dimensions of a giant. What made him appear large was the depth of his chest and the breadth of his heavily muscled shoulders.

"Well?" Long Rider asked in a measured voice. "Do you see 'em?"

Christopher Benton lowered his binoculars and shook his head. "It's as if that damned stallion has led his mares right into a mountain and is hiding from us."

"He's hiding, all right," Long Rider said. "But not in a mountain. Chris, my guess is that he's taken them up one of those big canyons to the northeast in the Bear River country."

Chris turned the binoculars to the northeast and did not speak for almost a full minute. "There are at least eight canyons up there, most of which—maybe even all—are boxes. Do you really think a mustang stallion as wily as Diablo would put himself and his band in that kind of trap?"

"I don't know," Long Rider admitted. "But he's out-guessed and outrun so many mustangers over the past couple of years that I wouldn't put anything past him. Horses, like people, can sometimes outsmart themselves."

Chris grinned. "Is that a little Oglala Indian folk wisdom, Gabe?"

"Nope. It's just my observation on men and horses."

"I couldn't argue with you on that," Chris said agreeably.

He and Long Rider had been friends for the past five years. Chris was an attorney specializing in land and water rights. He'd done well enough to buy a huge cattle ranch and hire Long Rider to manage it for him and his wife, Polly. Sometimes weeks would pass before Chris and Polly Benton could get out to their ranch from their town home in Ogden, but with Long Rider on the job, they never worried about their property or their cattle.

"Well," Gabe said, "it's up to you. Those badland canyons are almost a day's ride from here. And even after we get there, chances are that Diablo has outsmarted us and gotten away."

Chris looked up at the sky. There was a cold December

wind blowing plenty of snow up on the mountaintops. He turned up his fleece-lined leather coat. "I've been wanting that stallion ever since I laid eyes on him three years ago. Polly and I saw him on the very same day we bought the Rocking Horse Ranch, and that's when I promised her I'd catch, break, and ride that stallion before my thirty-third birthday. I'll be thirty-three at the end of January."

"If I were you," Gabe said, "it's a promise I'd forget."

"Why?"

"Because a stallion like that has got to be six or seven years old, at least."

"Then he's just reaching his prime," Chris argued. "In human years, he's probably still a little younger than I am."

"And full of piss and vinegar," Gabe said. "He's gonna be harder than those steel rails leading across the desert to California. He's gonna be meaner than a teased snake and far too set in his ways to ever become a saddle horse."

"Ah, come on! Aren't you exaggerating a little?"

"Nope," Gabe said, his smile dying. "That Appaloosa has had to fight other stallions and every other damn thing you can imagine to stay on top of the pack. He'd fight you, too, Chris. He'd be an animal you could never trust under the saddle, even if you did manage to catch and break him."

Chris put away his binoculars. "Gabe, you once admitted that all your adult life someone has tried to tell you what you can or can't do. You being a white boy raised by the Sioux, things haven't been easy, have they?"

Gabe's gray eyes tightened a little at the corners. "Life is a struggle. That's what separates the men from the pretenders. Neither I or my mother or the Indians that raised me ever expected things to be easy."

"Well," Chris said, "that being the case, why should you expect that I'd figure catching, breaking, and training that stallion would be easy? Fact of the matter is, the harder things come, the better we both appreciate them. And I already appreciate Diablo a hell of a lot.''

If Gabe hadn't cared for this man so much, he'd have dropped the argument right there, but he did care and that made him keep trying. ''A man with a wife and responsibilities needs to know his limitations, Chris.''

The attorney barked a strained laugh. ''Oh, so that's it! You're saying I'm not man enough to do the job?''

Gabe shook his head. ''I'm saying you've done right well by yourself for being only thirty-two. When I'm your age, all I'll have is a good horse, my saddle, and weapons. Maybe a few dollars in my Levi's. Not much more. You got a fine, big ranch, some nice cattle, and the prettiest wife in Utah Territory. So why not enjoy them? If you want a superior horse, you can afford to buy the best.''

''Wouldn't give me half the pleasure that Diablo would bring. And I never broke a mustang stallion before. Someday after Polly and I have children, I'd like to tell them how I did it. It'd be a story to be proud of.''

Gabe sighed with resignation. He was a man who loved challenges, too, but he was also a man who had responsibilities to nothing or no one. If he wanted to break a wild stallion and risk his neck, there wasn't a wife or child that would suffer if he got himself killed. With Chris, it was different.

''Stop worrying about me!'' Chris said, slapping the larger man on the shoulder. ''Catching that stallion is a dream of mine. Dreams almost never come true, but that doesn't mean they're any less real or valuable.''

Before Gabe could decide how to answer, Chris spurred his horse north.

''Might as well make up my mind to catch him,'' Gabe muttered as he gave his sorrel its head and let the animal run toward the canyons to the northeast.

• • •

They rode straight into the teeth of a freezing wind all afternoon, and by the time they reached the broken hills and the canyons up near the Bear River, both men were stiff with cold and a frigid sun was sliding into the western mountains.

"They're close," Gabe said, dismounting on wooden legs and crouching over the mustang's tracks. "I'd say that they passed this way less than two hours ago."

"Then let's follow them into the canyon and trap them!" Chris said, blowing to warm his frozen fingers. "If we wait until morning, they might escape in the night."

Gabe nodded. "You're the boss. But for my money, the thing to do is to track them to whichever canyon they went up and then make camp. If they're in a box canyon, they'll keep until morning, and if not, we've lost them anyway."

Chris considered this for almost a minute, and it was obvious to Gabe that his friend was pushing himself too hard. Chris was strong and tough—for a city man not accustomed to spending ten or twelve hours of every waking day in the saddle. He was the kind of man that didn't take no for an answer, and that made him push himself to the limit.

"You're one of the best trackers alive," Chris said finally. "You lead me to the right canyon and we'll take a look. If Diablo is in there, we'll try and figure a way to barricade the mouth and wait him out until morning. That fair enough?"

Gabe remounted. "Like I said, you're the boss. We'll do it your way."

"Cut the bullshit," Chris said with an uncharacteristic edge to his voice. "Out here, *you're* the boss. Hell, I know when to listen to someone who was born outdoors and raised by Indians. I'll never have half the feel for horses or wild country that you do. And I accept that. It's just that I have a feeling that we might finally have out-smarted Diablo.''

Chris took a deep breath. His face was pale and deter-mined. He looked exhausted and cold but his voice rang with conviction. "I want that stallion, Long Rider. I want him like I haven't wanted anything since Polly."

"Sure," Gabe said. "But the difference is, Polly wanted you in return. And she never had any intention of trying to stomp your guts out in a breaking corral. Understand?"

Chris chuckled. "Yeah. I understand. Let's catch that beautiful Appaloosa son of a bitch anyway. You lead, I'll follow."

Long Rider touched spurs to his sorrel's flanks and be-gan to track the mustang band. This was not the first time that he and Chris had hunted Diablo, and so he was very familiar with not only the stallion's hoofprints, but every mare in his band.

The tracks were easy to follow. Because snow had al-ready fallen and melted several times this past month, the ground was saturated and the hoof marks were embedded for anyone to see. The only problem they had was that the light was failing too quickly.

"There will be a half-moon up tonight," he said, push-ing his horse along. "If we don't find which canyon they're in by dark, I can still see the tracks well enough to go on."

"Let's just hope we don't have to go much farther," Chris said. "My butt has to be covered with saddle sores, and if I ever thaw out again, I'm sure that I'll feel them."

"Nobody said you had to leave that nice warm house of yours in Ogden and come out here to freeze your fanny off."

"Wouldn't miss it for the world," Chris muttered. "And I'd rather have my teeth chattering in the wintertime than be boiling out here in the summer."

Long Rider twisted around in the saddle. "You better seal those loose lips of yours. Your teeth sound like dice rattling around in a cup. Diablo is gonna think there's a crap game going on out here."

"Bullshit," Chris said with a weak smile. "Just find us the right canyon and let's make a fire and get warm!"

Long Rider wanted nothing more, but the stallion had led his mares on through the hills and past at least five canyons before finally turning into one. By then, it was dark and the temperature had plummeted well below the freezing point. Even worse, the wind had strengthened and it looked as if a storm was blowing down from the north.

"We may have to find a cave or some sort of shelter," Gabe said as he dropped from his saddle to peer up the dark canyon, where the fresh tracks of Diablo and his mares disappeared. "I got a feeling it's gonna start to snow within the next hour or two."

"If we go looking around for a cave—and that stallion is up there trapped in a box canyon—he might break out in the dark."

"That's possible."

"Then we'll make camp right here in the canyon's mouth," Chris said. "There's plenty of timber here-abouts. You can even show me how to fashion a Sioux shelter. You aren't going to let us freeze to death, are you?"

"Not me," Gabe said, pulling tighter the coat he'd made from his mother's tepee before she had been slaughtered by the white soldiers. "I'm wearing my buffalo robe coat."

"Yeah," Chris grumbled. "The one that you made from your mother's tepee. That's nice for you, but it don't do a thing for me."

"Let's get the wood burning and we can figure out what we're going to do next after we have a chance to thaw."

Chris nodded stiffly and they hurried to gather the abundant pine and cedar deadfall that lay close by. Gabe wasted no time in getting the fire started and while Chris was trying to get warm, he loosened the saddles on their horses and tied them to a picket line close to the wall, which formed half the mouth of the canyon.

"Here!" Chris said, digging into his saddlebags after they had both hunkered down beside the fire.

"What's this?" Gabe asked, holding a paper-wrapped bundle.

"It's a stuffed quail," Chris said. "One of Polly's little surprises."

Gabe unwrapped the paper and, sure enough, it was a quail. A big fat one with lots of seasoned stuffing jammed inside. "Well, I'll be damned. I was figuring we'd warm up a little cold jerky or maybe you'd bring a piece of beef, but nothing like this."

Gabe reached for a stick and skewered the quail. Chris followed his example, and within minutes the game birds were starting to smoke and cook. Gabe kept glancing up the dark canyon and wondering about the stallion.

"You think him and his mares are in there, admit it," Chris said, eyeing him across the flames.

"Yeah, for some reason, I do. I think he's up there and he's already smelled this meat cooking and he's trying to figure out what he's going to do next."

Chris peered into the darkness. "You think he'll try and stampede us tonight?"

"If he was a normal stallion, I'd say no. But this one is different. Mustangers say he thinks like an outlaw, and if you believe that is true, then he just might stampede us."

"So what can we do to stop him from trying it?"

"We build the fire up high and keep it up all night."

Long Rider studied the narrow canyon walls. "If it don't

snow so hard that it knocks the fire out, Diablo won't try to drive his band through and escape.''

Chris turned his bird on the stick and its fat leaked onto the flames, making sizzling sounds. ''Damn, I'm starting to feel my empty stomach,'' he complained. ''Must mean that the middle of me is starting to finally thaw.''

The attorney reached back inside his saddlebags and produced a pint of whiskey. He uncorked the bottle and raised it to Gabe. ''I know you don't drink, but I thought, under the circumstances, you might want to make this night an exception.''

''No, thanks,'' Gabe said.

''Are you sure? It'll warm your vitals.''

''I'm sure.''

Chris shrugged and took a long pull. He sighed and smacked his pale lips. ''Boy, that stokes a fire in a man's belly. How come you never drink?''

''Just doesn't do a thing for me,'' Gabe said with a shrug. ''Beside that, I've seen too many strong men made weak by whiskey. Indians as well as the whites. And I never seen a weak man made better by liquor. They just get foolish and then they get hurt or killed.''

Chris took another pull. ''You and the Mormons ought to get together and have a great time discussing the evils of demon rum and firewater.''

Gabe chuckled. ''They still after you and Polly to join their church?''

''They sure are. And if I didn't do so much legal work for the Union Pacific Railroad in Ogden, I'd probably either have to leave Utah or join 'em.''

Chris inspected his roasting bird and decided it was still too raw, so he put it back into the fire. ''They're pretty damn good people,'' Chris said. ''Hardworking, sober, and industrious.''

Gabe nodded in agreement. ''The main thing I do like

about them is that they take care of each other, like the Indian.''

The two men lapsed into silence and a few minutes later they were hungrily devouring their quail. Gabe could have eaten a second whole bird but he sure wasn't complaining.

''Damn tasty,'' he said. ''Where'd she get them?''

''At the butcher store in Ogden,'' Chris said. ''There's plenty of boys around Odgen who can shoot the eyes out of a grasshopper on the wing. They sell what they bag to the meat market. Tomorrow night, we'll each have ourselves a fat cottontail rabbit to roast.''

Gabe smiled. ''That wife of yours is something special, that's for certain.''

After they finished eating, both of them were reluctant to leave the fire and go out for more wood. But they did, and by the time it began to snow in earnest, their fire was blazing hot.

''You curl up as close as you can without catching fire and I'll take the first watch,'' Gabe said.

''Uh-uh,'' Chris said, objecting without much passion. ''The last time you took the first watch in a situation like this, you let me sleep the whole damn night.''

''I fell asleep, too,'' Gabe deadpanned. ''Woke up just a few minutes before you did.''

Chris stared and him and then he barked a laugh. ''I don't believe that for a minute, but I want to.''

''Then do,'' Gabe said. ''I'll wake you about three in the morning.''

''How you gonna know when it's three o'clock? You won't carry a watch and you sure won't see any stars up there this snowy night.''

''I'll just know,'' Gabe said.

The attorney stared at him for a moment, then said, ''Half-white, half-red, and the best of both, my friend. If it wasn't for you, I'd never be able to have a ranch to bring Polly to when city life and the law gets me down."

"It works good for me, too," Gabe admitted. "I got a ranch house all to myself and all the food I want. A few dollars in my pockets to spend in town on Saturday . . ."

"You been seeing a lot of that little schoolteacher out near Oreville, haven't you?"

Gabe ignored the remark. "Yes, sir," he said. "If it wasn't for you, I'd be somewhere else right now. Somewhere warm and comfortable instead of out here in a blizzard waiting to catch a killer stallion."

"Aw, come on," the attorney said, only half-serious. "You know we're both enjoying this."

"Glad to hear that," Gabe said. "Now, go to sleep and I'll enjoy it even more."

"You're a heartless bastard," Chris said. "You really know how to cut a friend to pieces with your cruel words."

"Go to sleep," Gabe said. "Three o'clock comes around pretty fast."

"Not on a night like this," Chris growled as he pulled a slicker close around him and toppled over onto his side, face to the flames.

Gabe watched his friend fall asleep almost instantly. Then he got up, fed the fire a few more logs, and went to his horse to get his rope and his rifle before he started into the canyon.

Maybe, if the canyon wasn't too deep, he'd catch a glimpse of Diablo and get a better idea of just what he was going to do when that big Appaloosa stallion decided there was no choice but to stampede out the way he'd come in—fire or no damn fire.

CHAPTER TWO

Gabe pulled his heavy buffalo robe tight around him and started up the canyon, not entirely sure what he was going to do if he did see the mustang band. The Appaloosa stallion had managed to gather eighteen or nineteen mares, and there would be several fillies and colts among them. It would be impossible to stop that many horses stampeding all at once if Diablo had really made his mind up about escaping the canyon.

Before Gabe had gone a half mile, the clouds broke to reveal the moon and a handful of cold stars. Gabe began to move very cautiously, using every rock and tree for cover. Fortunately, he was downwind of the mustangs, which would cancel out their excellent sense of smell. With any luck at all, he'd be on top of them before they could react. And, though it seemed a real longshot, Gabe had it in the back of his mind that he might even be able to rope the stallion and get him snubbed up to a tree.

But there was another part of Gabe that was almost hoping the Appaloosa would escape. It was such a magnificent

animal that it ought to be free, and most important, Gabe
was afraid that the powerful horse really would injure or
kill the stubborn attorney.

An hour after he had left the camp, Gabe sensed that
he was nearing the end of the canyon and that the mustangs were close. He also had decided that the reason the
Appaloosa had driven his mares into this particular canyon
was because it was boxed and therefore would offer the
best protection against the freezing north wind.

Crouched behind a rock, Gabe pulled his hands out of
his pockets and removed his gloves so that he would have
some control over the rope as he formed a loop. One thing
was sure: if he got within reach of Diablo, he would only
have one chance to make his throw, and the loop would
shoot as stiff as a strand of barbed wire.

Suddenly, he heard the stallion trumpet a warning that
could not have originated more than a dozen yards away.
Gabe peered up at the sky and saw the clouds skimming
toward a frozen moon.

It was now or never, and despite the numbing cold,
Gabe removed his heavy buffalo robe coat so that he would
be able to throw better and also move fast when Diablo
came after him. Once again the stallion trumpeted and
began to stomp its hooves in agitation. It had not seen or
smelled Gabe, but its sharp survival instincts were telling
the animal that danger was very close.

Long Rider stepped out in the open. The stallion saw
him and it had no fear of a man afoot. It charged through
its milling band, ears laid back, teeth bared to rip flesh.

Gabe waited until the very last moment, then he whirled
his rope once and let it fly. There was no time even to see
it settle over the stallion's head because Gabe leaped for a
nearby pine tree and managed to get just one twist of rope
around the tree before all hell broke loose.

Diablo struck the end of the rope moving like a runaway

train. And if the noose had not tightened just behind his jaws instead of farther down his powerful neck, it would have snapped like a piece of yarn.

Instead, the Appaloosa's head was yanked around so hard that the impact would have broken a normal animal's neck and killed it instantly. But the Appaloosa was no ordinary animal. It crashed to the earth stunned, but still game. Before it could recover and get back on its feet, Gabe pounced on its head. No horse could rise with its head pinned to the earth. Gabe covered the animal's head with his buffalo robe, snatched his knife from its scabbard and cut two short pieces from his rope. He used one to tie the buffalo robe around the stallion's head and he wound the other around Diablo's forefeet.

"Yaaaa!" he shouted at the mares and young horses, which had stampeded around them and were now racing for the mouth of the canyon.

Knowing Diablo was blinded and helpless, Gabe jumped for his rifle. He fired two warning shots and left the rest up to Chris Benton. If he heard the shots, the wisest thing that he could do would be to remain close beside the fire. The mustangs would not trample him or the fire if there was any way possible to get around it—and there was if they crowded through in single file.

But one thing was sure. Chris was in for a rude campfire awakening.

It was almost daylight before Chris found Long Rider pacing back and forth half-frozen before a small fire. Chris looked at the man and his brows were knit in anger until he saw Diablo on the ground. The stallion was dusted with a layer of snow. Despite the fact that his head was still covered by the heavy buffalo robe, he was so big and muscular that there was no doubting the fact that the famous Diablo had finally been caught.

"Well, I'll be damned," Chris said. "And I was all fixed to come up here and shoot you to death for stampeding those mustangs through our camp."

"I knew you'd keep your head and survive," Gabe said.

"I don't believe my eyes. You roped him?"

"I sure didn't tackle him," Gabe said, rubbing his hands briskly together.

Chris walked over to the stallion, which heard his footsteps crunch in the snow and started thrashing. The attorney retreated. "Holy smokes! I've seen him through the binoculars, but seeing him up close is another thing altogether, ain't it."

"Yeah," Gabe said. "So why don't you scratch him behind the ear and then we'll turn him loose. A horse like tha—"

"Will make the finest saddle animal west of the Mississippi River," Chris said. "Hell, Gabe, if we turn him loose, it's just a matter of time before some mustanger or angry rancher shoots him for stealing their mares. You know that! Or he'll be defeated by a younger stallion and maybe crippled so wolves or a cougar will pull him down."

"That's the way it's supposed to be," Gabe said quietly. "You can't change the nature of things."

"Once he's saddle broke, we could race him and win a lot of money."

Gabe's mouth twisted down at the corners. "You've already got plenty of money. And a wife who loves you and a body that still works. Set him free."

The attorney smiled. "I just can't. And as for the money, no one ever has enough. I realize that the Indian part of you disagrees, but it's the truth. Besides, if racing him is a bad idea, we could put him at stud. He's got champion bloodlines from someplace, Gabe. He'll bring top dollar at stud and he'll live a long and satisfying life with mares from near and far. Does that sound so bad?"

"It would to him," Gabe said. "He already gets all the lovin' he wants free. Now you want to be the one to decide when he can mount a mare and even which mare to mount. Don't seem to me he'll be anything but worse off."

Chris walked over and hunched down beside the fire. "My mind is made up, Gabe. That animal has eluded mustangers for years now, but it can't go on forever. Why, I've heard it said that his spotted hide alone is worth a hundred dollars! He's fast, but he can't outrun a long-range bullet. I'm saving him from a premature death."

"Seems to me," Gabe said, "he's done pretty well all by himself. And if he's as smart as I think he is, then he'll be moving on to a new territory this spring. You can't shoot what you can't see. I say we turn him loose."

"No!"

Gabe blinked and then his jawline hardened. "He'll never be a safe horse for man unless . . ." Gabe did not want to say it.

"Unless what!"

"Unless he's gelded, and I won't let you do that to him, Chris. It'd be like pulling the petals off a wildflower. He'd be half the animal he is now and we'd both hate ourselves. Do you understand me?"

Chris stared at the fire for a long time before he raised his head and looked Long Rider in the eye. "I want to ride him and breed him to a couple of our best mares. After that, we'll take him somewhere far away and turn him loose. He'll get himself a new harem and a fresh lease on life. What do you say? Will you help me?"

Gabe knelt down beside his friend. "All right," he said slowly. "But I break him, you ride him."

"No! I have to break him myself! You can show me."

Gabe wanted to grab his friend and employer by the throat and shake some sense into him, but he knew the man well enough to understand that the attorney's mind could never be changed.

"And you'll do everything I say?"

"Yeah. Everything."

"And if it doesn't work out after a few days we turn him loose?"

Chris reluctantly nodded. "Okay."

"And if it *does* work out, you ride him through Ogden, we breed him to a few of our best mares and he's freedom-bound this spring?"

"Yes, dammit!"

"All right, then," Long Rider said. "We'll get him to the ranch and start breaking him the same day."

Chris looked at the prostrate animal. "How are we going to get him to the ranch?"

"There are ways," Gabe said. "But we'll have to keep him blindfolded. In the meantime, I'd sort of like to wear my buffalo coat."

"I'll just bet you would!"

Chris smiled and clapped Gabe on the shoulders. "I know you don't like this, but thanks. Now let's get your buffalo robe off his head before you freeze to death and can't help me. I couldn't do it without you, Gabe. I expect you know that."

Long Rider dipped his chin. He did know it, and as he studied the once-proud mustang stallion lying helpless in the fresh snow, he also knew that this whole damn thing was a bad mistake.

CHAPTER THREE

When the storm passed and the sun lifted timidly above the eastern horizon, Gabe decided it was time to set about getting the stallion to Chris Benton's ranch.

"If you pull off that blinder, he's going to nail you for sure," Chris warned.

"That's right," Gabe said. "So we leave the blinder on. Also, we hobble those forelegs of his so that he can hop, but not run."

Chris was shocked. "He's going to hop blindfolded all the way back to my ranch? Hell, Gabe, that's a good forty miles!"

"I know exactly how far it is," Gabe said. "You're the one that insisted we have this party."

"But . . . well, isn't there some better way? Something a little less drastic."

Gabe shook his head. "Mustangers don't take chances and neither will we. And as far as being kind to this stallion, forget it. Understand that this mustang stallion will kill either one of us if he gets the slightest chance. He won't hesitate a second, because that's the rules he's always had to live by. If we coddle him, then we're just asking for big trouble.''

''Yeah, but forty miles! It might kill him.''

''No it won't,'' Gabe said. He took his rope and cut it to the right length, then fashioned the hobbes and tied them securely just above the fetlocks. ''If he breaks these, he'll run blind until he either runs headlong into something that kills him, or his heart explodes.''

Chris said nothing. His face was grim as he watched.

''If you think this is cruel,'' Gabe said, ''think again. Most mustangers slice the hamstrings so that their mustangs are permanently crippled. Not the good horses, but the ones that they ship east on the Union Pacific to be ground up for chicken feed or dog food. Other mustangers have been known to sew their mustangs' nostrils shut so they can't breathe properly. But the really bad ones . . .''

''All right, all right!'' Chris snapped. ''So we hobble Diablo's forelegs and keep him blindfolded until we get him into my breaking corral. Then what?''

''Then the real fun begins,'' Gabe said. ''But maybe by then you'll have a change of heart and turn him loose.''

Chris pivoted on his heel and went to his horse. ''We'll need my rope to lead him.''

''And what's left of mine as well,'' Gabe said. ''What we'll have to do is to keep him stretched between us. It's the only way. Without two ropes around him, even blindfolded and hobbled, he'd stampede right over the top of one of us.''

Chris studied the Appaloosa with a troubled expression. He opened his mouth to say something, then shut it and remained silent as he untied his lariat from his saddle and handed it to Gabe, who managed to slip it around Diablo's neck without getting pawed by the stallion's sharp front hooves.

"Stand back," Gabe warned. "I'm cutting the short tie around his fetlocks. He'll come up in a big hurry."

Chris mounted his horse, taking his rope and dallying it around his saddle horn. "You're gonna make a jump for your own saddle, right?"

"That's right. And the moment Diablo is on his feet, he'll try to run and then he'll crash down hard. Give him slack."

Chris nodded. He watched Long Rider cut the short rope and vault into his saddle as Diablo surged to his feet. The huge stallion was furious. He squealed and tried to run and crashed down hard, jerking the rope out of Chris's hand.

The attorney cursed and started to leap off his horse, but Gabe saw him in time and shouted, "Stay where you are!"

"But my rope!"

"Leave it!"

Chris nodded stiffly as Diablo squealed and came back to his feet. Gabe still had his own rope around the stallion's neck but it was shorter than he would have liked. When Diablo stuck the rope again, he went down a third time.

"He's gonna kill himself!" Chris shouted.

"Then, dammit, turn him loose! This is just the start of it," Gabe said coldly.

Chris Benton shook his head and Gabe held on. "Now grab your rope."

Chris rode in, jumped to the ground, picked up the rope, and was back on his horse in the blink of an eye as Diablo struggled to stand. The stallion's forelegs were already rope burned and bloodied. The powerful animal shook its head trying to rid itself of the blindfold.

"He's smart," Gabe said, noting how the mustang realized it was helpless as long as it was blind. "Now slowly back your horse up until the rope is tight. I'll do the same.''

They both backed their horses up and Diablo began to thrash against the pressure.

''Come forward a step!'' Gabe shouted. ''Let's give him a little more slack. That's it.''

Diablo stopped fighting the rope. He stood with his hobbled forelegs braced wide apart. His flanks heaved and his speckled hindquarters quivered with anger or fear or maybe a little of both.

''What do we do now?'' Chris asked in a worried voice.

''Not a damn thing until we see what he's going to do.''

They waited almost five minutes while the stallion gathered his strength, and then he charged blindly at Chris and his horse. Gabe's rope took the full force of the stallion's charge and his big sorrel gelding almost squatted down in the dirt, burying its hind feet into the soft ground and trying to keep from being dragged down.

''Move!'' Gabe shouted. ''But keep your rope.''

Chris reined hard and drove his spurs into his horse's flanks. The animal jumped forward, and when it hit the end of the rope it threw Diablo off balance and the stallion slammed back to the earth.

Long Rider was getting angry. ''Chris, you ready to let him go yet?''

''No!''

''Then put some tension in your rope.''

''I am.''

Diablo lay on the ground, striking his head against the spongy earth. Long Rider watched with sadness. He wondered if the Appaloosa stallion would beat its own brains out rather than give in to its tormentors. Gabe remembered how he had once found himself locked in the white man's dark prison cell, without hope or even understanding of why he had been wronged.

A barred cell had given him a terrible feeling, but he had never tried to kill himself and he had always believed that one day he would be free again. And now, as Diablo stopped beating its head against the earth, it occurred to Gabe that perhaps the Appaloosa felt the same way. That it hadn't given up, but was simply waiting for its chance. A chance that would most certainly come sooner, if not later.

"He's given up!" Chris shouted. "Maybe he realizes it's hopeless to fight."

Gabe said nothing. Diablo had too much heart to give up. He was just biding his time. The wild, wasted thrashing was over. Now, the deadly waiting game had begun.

"Give him slack," Gabe called. "Let's get him on his feet and moving toward the ranch."

Chris nodded and moved his horse in a little. "How's this?"

"Good. Now let's teach him how to be led."

Diablo seemed to understand right away what was being demanded of him. The horse barely struggled and began to hop forward. It was painful to watch and yet also very beautiful because the Appaloosa was such a magnificent piece of horseflesh. Still, their progress was slow and it took them nearly a half hour to get out of the canyon.

"At this rate," Chris said, "we won't get back to the ranch until spring."

Gabe had to agree. "We'll see how he's doing this afternoon. If I can get away with loosening his hobbles so that he can shuffle those front feet, then I will. There's a chance we can remove the hobbles altogether in the next day or two."

"Can we get rid of that damned blindfold?" Chris asked.

"No. If he can see us, we're in trouble. The blindfold

stays on until we get him saddled and you hop on his back.''

Chris looked so worried that Gabe added, ''Unless you've changed your mind and want me to break him.''

''I'll do it,'' Chris said stubbornly. ''I'm the one that's going to ride him through Ogden.''

Gabe did not argue any more because that only seemed to stiffen the man's resolve to be foolish. Instead, he kept a close eye on Diablo and kept the stallion moving.

That night, neither one of them slept more than an hour or two as Diablo whinnied for his band of mares. The next morning, Gabe managed to swing his horse around the stallion and cut its legs out from under the animal. When it was down, he jumped on its head again and shouted, ''Loosen the hobble!''

Chris was at his side in just a moment. ''How much?''

''Couple inches.''

Diablo lay very still. His flesh quivered until Chris untied the hobble rope knot, and the instant he felt the tension give way, he pawed with his front legs and caught Chris in the left arm and knocked him flying.

''Ahhh!'' Chris gritted as he grabbed his arm. ''He broke it!''

Gabe swore to himself and somehow managed to refasten the hobble rope and yell, ''Get back on your horse!''

When Chris, white faced and in obvious pain, did finally remount, Gabe jumped away from the stallion and threw himself into the saddle as Diablo climbed back on his feet, tried to run, and then stopped.

Gabe, in his haste and concern for Chris, had given the stallion too much play. ''Can you hold him from your end? If you can't, I'm turning him free.''

''I can hold him!''

''Then back your horse up and let's keep some tension on the rope.''

Chris's left arm dangled at his side and he used his right to back his horse and somehow keep his dally.

"All right," Gabe said. "Let's just hold still for a minute. How bad is your arm?"

"It ain't too bad," Chris gritted. "I've broke it before."

"It's not splintered through the skin?"

"No," Chris said. "This heavy coat saved me."

Gabe expelled a sigh of relief. "I think we ought to let him go right now and get you back to the ranch."

"Not a chance! We got this far, we aren't quitting now."

"You're more stubborn than a Missouri mule," Gabe said with exasperation as he reined his sorrel gelding south, leaving the Bear River country behind.

If Diablo cooperated, it would take them two more days to reach Benton's ranch. Once there, Gabe figured he could ride for Ogden and a doctor. He had a feeling that Chris wasn't going to be wanting to make the ride himself.

"Polly is going to be pretty upset about this," Chris said, breaking into Long Rider's thoughts. "But I'll make it clear that you objected from the start."

"I'd appreciate that," Gabe said. "That wife of yours does have a temper. I'd like to keep on the right side of her if I can."

"Hell," Chris replied, "she's secretly in love with you as it is. If you'd been a man who wanted to plant roots and make a place for himself, you could have had her."

"She got the best man."

"She got the one that can make the money," the attorney said, trying to laugh. "As far as being the 'best,' well, that would be a matter of considerable debate. You're one of the only truly free men I've ever known, and you have that Indian code of morality that I admire."

"You're honest."

"Yeah, yeah I am," Chris said. "But I work the angles

and I make compromises every day in order to keep paying the bills. I doubt you even know the word *compromise.*''

Gabe just smiled and looked up at the sky. The storm had passed but it was still mighty cold and it would drop below freezing again tonight. ''White lawyer talk too damn much sometimes.''

Chris chuckled. ''White man may talk too much, but he is also a man of action. You just wait and see me when I ride this outlaw.''

''It had better be after that arm is healed,'' Gabe said. ''If either Polly or I catch you messin' around with Diablo before that, then I'll turn the horse loose.''

Chris's smile slipped. ''A broken left arm won't hurt my riding.''

Gabe scowled. Maybe Polly could reason with her husband, but Gabe wasn't having much luck.

CHAPTER FOUR

By the time they finally approached the Benton ranch, it had begun to storm again and it was all Chris could do to stay erect in his saddle the last few miles. Gabe did everything possible to keep the Appaloosa stallion under control. If it had not been blindfolded, the mustang would have realized how easy it would have been to rush Chris and his horse and knock them both down. With only one horse and rope, he would have had a very good chance of attacking Gabe, injuring his gelding and escaping.

But Diablo *was* blindfolded, and when they finally arrived at the ranch, Polly sized up things immediately and ran to open the corral gate. It was heavy, but she pulled it open as if it were nothing, and then stood anxiously as snow began to cover her pretty face.

"What happened?" she cried, having the good sense not to rush in between men and horses.

"We'll tell you later," Chris shouted over the wind. "Get inside and get some hot coffee brewing!"

"Coffee has been boiling for two days waiting on you. I'm not going back inside until you both come with me!"

Neither Chris nor Gabe dared to argue with Polly Benton. She had a little upturned nose, dark curls and dimples. She looked like a pixie and did not stand over five feet tall, but she had more energy, grit, and determination than three ordinary women.

Dressed in one of her husband's heavy-weather coats, she looked like a rumpled child. "I was ready to saddle a horse and come looking for you in this storm. You both must be frozen!"

Gabe led Diablo into the breaking corral and dropped his rope. He rode his staggering sorrel gelding back out of the corral, then dismounted to slam and bar the heavy gate.

"Do you have to leave the blindfold on him?" Polly asked. "Maybe I could . . ."

"Don't even think about it," Gabe said. "Besides, when he's got a few minutes by himself, he'll easily be able to rub that blindfold away."

"You think the corral will hold him?" Chris asked, dropping weakly to his feet as Polly rushed to his side and gave her injured husband support.

"Yeah. I buried new posts four feet in the ground this fall. Besides that, even the wildest horse won't attack a solid wall."

This particular breaking corral had been built and designed by Long Rider himself. It was solid to a height of nearly eight feet, but there was a sixteen-inch gap between the bottom of the fence and the earth, just enough for a downed man to wiggle through if a stallion like Diablo was after him. It was round, some fifty feet in diameter. In a round corral, a bronc could not back into a corner and defend himself. Also, he couldn't slam into corners and weaken the corner posts.

"Look at him," Chris said. "I never seen a finer animal in my life."

Polly, who was a good horsewoman, was not so impressed. "Is he the reason your left arm is dangling from your side? Oh, Chris, what happened? Why did you bring a killer like that back here? He deserves to be running free on the range!"

"Now don't *you* start that," Chris said angrily. "I've been listening to Long Rider for the last three days. And I'm tired of it!"

Chris pushed his wife away and took his horse to the barn.

Polly looked up at Gabe, a question in her eyes.

"He's hurtin'," Gabe said, trying to explain the man's curt behavior. "He's in pain and he's weak from hunger and lack of sleep. It's been a rough trip. Damned rough."

Polly nodded with understanding. "It was crazy to go north into the Bear River country at this time of year. You could have gotten yourselves snowed in and caught up in a real bad fix."

"We'd have pulled out before that."

"I don't believe it," Polly said. "Chris has never had any sense when it comes to mustanging. I wish you could have talked him out of catching that horse. He's wanted Diablo for years, and for just as long I've been praying he'd never be caught. And I'll bet I have you to thank for this."

"He's the boss, Polly. He'd never by happy until he caught that horse. I was hoping he'd turn him loose after a little while."

"But he hasn't."

"No," Gabe said. "But maybe you can talk sense into him. Right now, though, I'd better get along because he's going to need some help to unsaddle. He broke his left arm."

"Damn," she said. "I was afraid you were going to say that. I'll go make the coffee and get some hot food on the stove."

"Thanks," Gabe said, pulling his Stetson down against the wind. "And I sure liked that stuffed quail and that rabbit."

Polly turned. The snow was melting on her cheeks like running tears. "As soon as you have rested and eaten, you'd better ride for a doctor."

"I set the arm," Gabe said. "I don't think it's a bad break. Just sort of swollen up and purple. Probably hurts like hell."

"Please go for the doctor anyway. Dr. Wheeler is having a hard time paying his bills and he could use the business. And I don't want to take any chances of a bone infection."

"I'll do it," Gabe promised.

Gabe did not wait out the storm but rode for Ogden just as soon as he had had his fill and could catch and saddle a fresh mount.

When Chris learned that his friend was leaving right away to get a doctor, he was angry. "Dammit, Gabe! I don't need to see a doctor! You set this arm as well as any sawbones."

"I'd like to make sure," Gabe said. "Doc Wheeler has had a lot more practice than I have."

"At least wait out the storm!"

"Can't do that," Gabe said, jamming his boot into a stirrup and hoisting himself up into the saddle.

"If the storm gets worse, you lay over until it gets better," Polly said. "I want you to make me that promise."

"All right," Gabe said.

"Wouldn't hurt you to rest over in Oreville a night,

anyway," Chris said. "That schoolteacher could warm you up tonight."

"Chris!" Polly scolded. "You mind your tongue."

The attorney managed a weak grin. "As long as you're in Ogden, why don't you stop by my office and check the mail? Tell my secretary that I'll be in next week sometime to catch up on things."

"With that bad arm, you might as well go in sooner," Polly said.

Gabe left before they started to wrangle and the day got colder. It was late in the afternoon and the sky looked bad. He figured that a foot of snow had fallen in the last few days and there was more to come.

Maybe he would spend the night in town. But tomorrow, the next day at the latest, he'd return. There was a lot of work to be done on this ranch even in winter. Cattle and horses to be fed and ice to be broken through in the water troughs. One thing was for sure; Chris would not be in any shape to work.

Gabe rode through the little town of Oreville without stopping to see Miss Betsy Rogers, though when he passed her one-room schoolhouse he saw her standing in front of the class. She was a good teacher, he was sure of that much. It reminded him how very fortunate he was to be able to read himself.

His father, whose name had been Adam, had been killed by the Sioux when he foolishly led a few wagons into the Black Hills of South Dakota seeking gold. His mother, Amelia, had been spared and taken as a squaw before Gabe was born. By the time he could crawl, he was looked upon by the Oglala Sioux as one of their own. And indeed, except for the fact that his hair was the color of sand and his eyes were gray, he had never been aware of any difference between himself and the other children of the tribe.

His had been a wonderful and exciting childhood. He had learned the Indian way and taken to it naturally. His father, Little Wound, had been both wise and kind. He raised Gabe as if he were his own flesh and blood and had treated Gabe's mother with respect and deep affection. By the time Gabe was old enough to join the warriors on a buffalo hunt, he had known that his mother had completely accepted the Indian way and had no desire to leave the Sioux people.

Amelia had secretly taught her only son how to read and write. She had managed to save her Bible, and it was from the verses and psalms that Gabe had learned his words and letters. He had also learned much about his mother from the thoughts she had left him in the margins of the Bible. Now, years after her death, he still treasured and read her Bible just as he wore her tepee buffalo robe coat as a constant reminder of her love and courage.

Through the falling snow, Gabe saw Oreville, which was locked in winter just like the rest of Utah Territory. There were few people moving around outside. This was a mining town and they would be operating underground in any weather, but out in the street, hardly anything moved.

Pulling his collar closer around his face, Gabe rode on to Ogden. That railroad town was far bigger and only seven miles to the south, but in this freezing weather, it seemed much farther.

When he finally did arrive at Ogden, it was just as the westbound Union Pacific train was pulling out of its depot and heading for California. Gabe watched the faces of passengers through the windows. He had never quite been able to accept how many whites there were—so many that you saw some of them and knew that there was no way you would ever see that particular person again in this world. It had never been that way when he had been raised by the Indians.

He tied his horse at the hitching rail in front of Doc Wheeler's office. A couple of freight wagons were moving on the streets, but not much else. The snow was falling harder now and the temperature seemed to have dropped a few more degrees.

Gabe stomped his boots on the boardwalk to rid them of crusted snow before he opened the door to the doctor's office. When he entered, the hot air of the room almost buckled his knees and he saw the doctor feeding more wood into the potbellied stove.

"What are you trying to do, sweat the poison out of your patients?" Gabe asked. He and the doctor were friends and Wheeler was always teasing him about the Indians' *initi*, or sweat lodges.

Dr. Dave Wheeler was in his early fifties. He was pudgy and rumpled and very good at what he did. Best of all, he didn't take himself too damned seriously as most physicians Gabe had met were inclined to do.

"Hell no! I'm just trying to keep warm. Maybe if folks learn it's warm in here, they'll come and pay me a visit. Once I get 'em in my chair, I can always come up with something that ails them so I can prescribe a powder and collect a fee."

Gabe chuckled. "The old Indian medicine men I knew sort of had the same idea. Nothing easier than making a cure on an ailment that never existed except in the patient's mind."

"You got that figured out right," Wheeler said. "What are you doing riding to town on a day as miserable as this one?"

"I come to ask you to ride out to the Benton ranch. Chris got himself kicked by a stallion and his arm is broken."

"How long ago?"

"Three days."

"You set the bone?"

"I did," Gabe replied. "Wasn't a bad break but Miss Benton would still like you to take a look. Chris is in pain."

"I'll be in pain as well before I reach the ranch in this weather. You coming back with me?"

"I have to go by Mr. Benton's office and check his mail, then I'll accompany you back as far as Oreville."

The doctor winked. "Ahh, I forgot! You and that pretty schoolteacher have been causing tongues to wag. You know, it's a secret from most folks, but Betsy Rogers has been married twice already. That woman is figuring to lasso you for number three."

"She knows better," Gabe said. "I'm just someone in between."

"Good thing you have a meeting of the minds."

Gabe left the doctor a few moments later and promised to meet him outside after he packed his medical bag and a few things for an overnight stay. It was obvious that the doctor was happy to be leaving, even if it did mean facing a snowstorm for a few cold hours of riding. The doctor liked Chris and Polly and they always had a good visit.

Gabe checked Chris's mail, stuffed a few letters that did not look very important into his pockets, then joined Wheeler and rode out. Altogether, he had not been in Ogden more than an hour.

At Oreville, Gabe parted company with Wheeler. The man was riding in a covered surry that did offer some protection from the snow, and the roads were passable.

"Tell everyone I'll be along tomorrow sometime. What day is this?"

"Friday."

Good, he thought, that means that Betsy won't have to teach tomorrow morning and we can enjoy ourselves most of Saturday.

"Quit smiling!" the doctor said angrily. "I can read your evil mind."

Gabe said nothing as he turned his horse up the snowy street toward the little white house were Miss Betsy Rogers resided all by herself.

CHAPTER FIVE

Long Rider piled off his horse and tied it under a shed no longer in use. He stripped his saddle and carried it through the snow up to the back door, which he opened into a little laundry room.

"Betsy?"

He heard a noise and then a man shout, "It's time we settled this thing once and for all!"

Long Rider started to turn and leave. After all, he only saw Betsy Rogers once or twice a week and there were no ties between them. Betsy was looking for a husband and Gabe had made it very clear that he had no intention of getting serious.

As Gabe kicked open the back door and started toward the shed, he suddenly felt a sharp pain in the back of his neck. The next thing he knew, he was facedown in the snow with someone on top of him beating the bejesus out of the back of his head.

"Stop it, Ronald, you're going to kill him!" Betsy cried.

"Son-of-a-bitchin' Indian lover, I'll do the territory of Utah a big favor!"

Betsy screamed but her words were caught up by the wind, and Gabe was already twisting his powerful body and dumping the man off his back. He felt weak and dizzy and when he saw the bloody butt of the man's pistol, he knew he'd been viciously pistol-whipped.

Ronald was big and he was enraged. He came at Gabe with that damned pistol slashing, and Long Rider was still too dazed to react quickly. He barely managed to get his hand up and partially deflect the blow, but the weapon opened a gash across his cheekbone.

Betsy threw herself on Ronald and bit his wrist, trying to make him drop the gun. Her teeth must have sank deep because the man bellowed with pain and knocked her to the snow, then snarled and lunged at Gabe.

Gabe struck out with his left, a good straight jab in the teeth that other men had told him felt like getting hit by the end of a fence post. This time was no different. Ronald was stopped cold in his tracks and both of his lips were crushed to pulp.

Gabe lunged at the man and knocked him sideways, then jumped on him and grabbed his throat with one hand and smashed his face with the other. He hit him twice more; huge, savage blows that broke Ronald's nose and opened a nasty gash across his brow.

Betsy was back on her feet pleading, only this time, it was for Long Rider to have mercy.

"Please," she begged, "can't you see that he's finished? You'll kill him!"

Gabe's powerful fingers tightened on the man's throat until his eyes bulged and his tongue protruded in a silent cry. He shook Ronald and hissed, "I was *leavin'*, mister. I had my back to you and I was going out her door! You had no damn call to pistol-whip me!"

The man gagged and tried to shake his head. His face was as purple as a grape.

"Get out of here!" Gabe hissed. "And don't you ever come back again! Hear me?"

The man gagged something unintelligible and Gabe climbed off his chest and helped him to his feet, then gave him a hard shove. Ronald lost his footing and landed in a dead flower bed. He scrambled back up to his feet and raced headlong for the front gate.

Gabe watched him disappear in the falling snow and then walked back to his fallen saddle, picked it up, and started for the shed and his horse. He figured he'd overtake Doc Wheeler and be back at the ranch by ten o'clock.

"Gabe, please! Come back here!" Betsy cried. "You're hurt!"

"I'll live," he growled.

"Dammit, I fought for you! You can't just ride out half-dead in a snowstorm! Now be sensible!"

Gabe threw his saddle blanket over his horse's back, but Betsy grabbed it and yanked it off and pitched it in the snow shouting, "You aren't going out in this storm all bloodied like this!"

"You must be forgetting I'm not one of your pupils," he grated. "But even so, I got a lesson here tonight, and the lesson was that I don't need a woman that's going to be having jealous boyfriends crazy enough to kill a man."

"He's *not* my boyfriend!"

Gabe turned on her. Betsy was thirty and full-bodied. "He sure acted like a boyfriend to me."

"Well . . . well he just thinks he is," she said lamely. "Ronald has a temper."

"It'll get him killed if he ever tries to lay a hand on me again," Gabe warned. "And I'm no half-breed, though I'd be pleased if I was."

Her face softened. She would have been beautiful if it

hadn't been for a childhood accident that had broken her nose. Someone hadn't had the guts to set it properly and it had healed crooked. But she had a nice smile and the bluest eyes Gabe had ever seen. She was also bright and had strong principles about right and wrong. Betsy's pupils adored her but thought she was too strict, and their parents admired her because she could produce amazing results in her classroom. Gabe had heard it said many times that Betsy had a gift for teaching rarely seen and seldom appreciated. But most important to Gabe, Betsy was a woman who genuinely loved to make love.

"Please come inside," she said. "I was trying to get rid of Ronald. He'd been after me for weeks to go to a dance tonight and . . . well, you haven't been around and I was starved for some company. I wouldn't have stayed with him very long. I just had to go out tonight. We were about to leave when you came in the back door and Ronald had been drinking a little and . . . well, you know the rest."

Gabe nodded. His head was beginning to throb and he felt chilled to the bone. The idea of galloping back to the ranch was something he did not relish.

"I'll build a fire," she said, "and because you smell like you haven't bathed in about three months, I'll scrub your back while you take a nice hot bath."

"I could use a little scrubbing, I guess."

"Of course you could. And I'll cook a roast and pie and when you're clean, shaven, and full of good food, we'll go to bed and I'll make you very glad that you were wise enough to stay."

Betsy kissed his good cheek. "Now, how does that sound?"

Gabe's anger melted like icicles in April. "It sounds like dyin' and going to the white man's heaven," he said. "Or the Indian's happy hunting ground."

Betsy retrieved his blanket while he picked his saddle back off the ground and followed the woman inside.

She lived up to her promises. Two hours later, Gabe felt halfway human again. He'd been washed and scrubbed, fed, and escorted into the bedroom.

"Come here," he said, reaching for her.

Betsy undressed slowly, knowing he liked to see her body. She was proud of her figure and enjoyed showing it off to a man who had a good eye. And Long Rider's eye was very good.

"Are you sure you feel up to this?" she asked, sweeping her hands down before herself after she had peeled off the last garment.

"You bet I do," he said.

Betsy slipped into the bed beside him. Despite the fire, it was still chilly in the bedroom and they came together tight, both enjoying the feel of each other's body heat.

He kissed her lips and she responded eagerly, pushing her tongue into his mouth as his hands rubbed her back and then slid down to the roundness of her thighs and buttocks. Her legs parted slightly and his fingers probed until she sighed with pleasure.

"Oh, you really are something, Gabe. Just have your way with me."

"I will," he said, slipping his finger into her wet honey pot and wiggling it until her hips began to rotate and lift to the pressure of his long middle finger.

Gabe moved his finger in and out until she was wet and ready inside, and then rolled over and mounted her hard and sudden, the way she liked.

Betsy moaned as he raised himself up and began to move on her. Slow and easy but deep enough that she began to pant and squirm.

"Oh," she whispered, "harder. I want it hard to-night!"

"I aim to please," he said, grinding down on her as her heels raked the sheets and she clung to him.

She was a strong woman and even though he was exhausted, Gabe found himself renewed in her hot, fluid embrace. He concentrated in pleasing her first, because he knew that he would erupt inside of her like a fire hose when he lost control.

"Yes!" she cried.

Gabe laughed deep in his chest and drove the schoolteacher half-crazy. When she started to thrash and rake his back with her nails, he began to drive straight in and out of her.

Suddenly, Betsy's body stiffened and he felt her start to buck under his weight. She cried out and her hips could not stop slamming at his hips. Gabe dropped his weight down on her and then sank his big rod to the hilt and filled her with his seed while she moaned and clawed like a wildcat.

Afterward, they rested in each other's arms until Gabe was limp and rolled off her to sleep.

Betsy, however, was much too aroused for sleep. "I know how tired you are. I can feel your ribs and you've even lost weight. But even knowing all that, I may not be able to help myself from ravaging your wonderful body. You do something that brings out the animal in me."

"For that," he said sleepily, "I will always be grateful. This is your bed. If you can get a rise out of me, then go ahead and climb on. But I might not be up to my standards tonight. I'm running a little low on sleep."

"We can sleep all day tomorrow in between lovemaking," she said, rising up and studying his lacerated cheek. "Damn that stupid Ronald, anyway. I'm glad you broke his nose."

"Good," he said.

Betsy rolled over to study her clock. "Midnight," she said after a few moments. "I'm coming after you again at midnight."

But Gabe didn't hear her. He was already asleep.

CHAPTER SIX

Gabe felt Betsy's body begin to quake like an aspen, and then she cried out in ecstasy as he emptied his seed inside of her with all his raw animal power. For several moments, neither of them spoke as they waited for their hearts to slow and their breath to return.

"That makes seven times we've done it since I got here last night," Gabe said. "If we don't stop, you won't be able to walk into your classroom on Monday."

"If we don't stop," she said, "I might just die a happy and satisfied woman. Gabe, why don't you quit the ranch and move into town? I know you could find work here, and together we could have such a good time."

He rolled off her. "I like ranching better than anything except hunting, fishing, and making love to you. Though I think I've got the order turned around backward."

"But we could do this *all* the time!" She reached for his still-hard manhood. "I would put a perpetual smile on your lips, Long Rider."

"At this rate, we'd screw each other down to a nub,"

he said, trying to keep things light. "Why don't we let things ride the way they are between us? There's nothing that needs fixing."

Betsy sat up and pulled on her robe. Her smile was gone and her eyes looked sad. "People gossip terribly in a small town like Oreville," she said. "And because I'm a schoolteacher, they're getting upset about you and me."

"Ignore them," Gabe said shortly.

"Ignore them?" Betsy shook her head. "I knew that's what you'd tell me to do. It's what you'd do. But I'm *not* you, Gabe. I need this job and I need . . . well, I need respectability."

"And you can't have that with a man like me stopping in for a couple nights a week. Is that it?"

"You *must* understand."

"I sure do," Gabe said. "I've often wondered why you've put up with the arrangement this long."

"Because . . ." She had trouble saying it. "Because I'm in love with you. And because no man has ever made love to me the way you have. And I've had a few men."

"And two husbands?"

"Yes. Both bastards and wife beaters. You're so different from either one of them that I find it impossible to let you go. And yet, if I'm going to be asked back next year by the school board . . ." She let her words trail away.

Gabe sat up and reached for his underclothes, knowing it was time to go away for keeps. "I understand. And I guess I've been thinking of my own needs more than yours. The truth of it is that you do deserve a good man who will give you his name and be home to keep you company every night—but not one like that Ronald character."

"No, of course not."

Gabe pulled on his pants and buckled them, then reached for his boots and stockings and got them on as he spoke. "If it means anything to you, I love you, too, Betsy.

And if you are ever in trouble, just send for me. No matter where I am, I'll come and help.''

Betsy's face crumpled and she covered it with her hands and sobbed. ''Oh, dammit! I knew it had to end someday. I told myself over and over it did, and I tried to prepare myself for it but I failed.''

Gabe took her into his arms. ''You didn't fail at anything. I love you, your pupils love you . . .''

''They *hate* me!''

''They respect you,'' Gabe said. ''That's the most important thing.''

Betsy sniffled. ''I am a good teacher and I love those children. If they weren't so important, I'd say the hell with the school board. But teaching is such a big part of my life. On Saturdays and Sundays, when I'm not teaching, if you aren't with me, I feel lost. I can hardly wait to go back to the class on Monday.''

Gabe understood completely. ''Betsy, I feel pretty much that way about mustanging and ranching and just getting on a horse and going nowhere in particular. I'm too footloose to ever settle in one place for too long. Why, right now, I've even been thinking of leaving the Benton ranch and riding up to the Dakotas. I've some friends there and some places to see.''

Betsy sniffled as she got dressed. Gabe watched, feeling a sense of loss, a sense of something ending that had to end but did not feel good. He was about to put on his own shirt when there was a loud knock at the front door.

Betsy, still only half-dressed, froze. ''Now, who could that be?''

''Gabe! Gabe, are you in there?''

''It's Polly,'' he said, hurrying to the door. ''She wouldn't come here unless it was an emergency.''

Gabe yanked open the door and Polly threw herself against his bare chest and he felt the wetness of her tears against his skin even as a chill of dread filled his heart. "Something has happened to Chris. What is it?"

She looked up and it seemed to Gabe that Polly had suddenly grown old. "He's been stomped by Diablo. He's hurt real bad. We rushed him into town and he's asking for you."

The muscles of Gabe's face stretched out like pieces of rawhide under his flesh and he blinked. "Where is he?"

"At Doc Wheeler's office. He was there when it happened or Chris would already be dead. The doctor is going to try and operate and stop Chris from bleeding inside."

The ride to Ogden seemed to take an eternity, but finally they reached the snow-covered street in front of the doctor's office. Crashing inside, Gabe rushed into a second room and came to an abrupt halt.

Doc Wheeler was examining Chris, and when he turned and saw Gabe, he shook his head and said, "You can have a few minutes with him. He wants to talk to you and then see Polly."

"What about the operation?"

Again, the doc shook his head. "I'll be just outside. Don't take long."

Gabe felt his heart drop to his feet. The meaning was terribly clear. Chris was dying and there was no hope in an operation.

"How you doin'?" Gabe asked, taking the young attorney's hand and trying to dredge up a smile.

Chris's eyes fluttered open. "I wanted to give Diablo some grain and water. I slipped in the snow and he was on me like a mountain cat. He's fast."

"I'll turn him loose or shoot him after I've had some time to think about it."

"Set him free," Chris whispered. He was very pale and his cheeks and eyes appeared to be sunken into the hollows of his face. He had looked wan and haggard when Gabe had seen him last after racing to Ogden for the doctor; now he looked ghastly.

"Gabe, listen to me carefully. I'm worried about Polly and the ranch."

"I'll take care of them both," Gabe promised.

"Yeah, I know that, but there's a mortgage. A big mortgage that has to be paid every month, and the ranch doesn't have enough cattle to handle it."

Gabe tried to hide his surprise. "But you told me it was paid for."

"It was, but I stupidly put a mortgage on the place to invest in some mining stock that went bad. I could have paid it off from my law practice, but now . . ." Tears filled Chris's eyes. "Now I don't know what's going to happen."

"It will work out," Gabe said. "Right now the only thing that's important is you getting well again."

"Cut the bullshit," Chris said weakly. "We both know I'm finished."

He gripped Long Rider's wrist. "Talk to the banker, Mr. Dalton Kimbal. He'll think of a way to save the ranch. Talk to him, Gabe!"

"I will."

"And don't say anything to Polly about this until . . . later. She's got enough grief to . . ."

Chris couldn't finish as a powerful spasm shook his body and left him trembling and spent.

"Doc!"

Dr. Wheeler and Polly rushed inside. Polly took one glance at her husband and burst into tears. The doctor touched Gabe's arm and then stepped out of the examining room.

"He's almost gone," Wheeler said.

"And there's nothing you could do?"

"No. I could open him up, but why? I'm a country

doctor and a good one, but I'm not a surgeon and I'll not put a man through more agony than he's already trying to endure."

Gabe nodded and dropped his hands to his sides in hopeless futility. "Dammit, I should have insisted we turn that stallion loose! If I hadn't caught him, Chris would be fine right now."

"It's not your fault," the doctor said. "Before he went out to that corral and was stomped, you should have seen him. He was in pain from his arm, but very, very happy about capturing Diablo. He laughed and even bragged as how you'd probably wind up breaking him and he'd get all the credit."

Gabe felt miserable. Maybe the doctor was right, but that didn't ease the pain he was feeling inside.

"Oh, no!" Polly cried. "No, no!"

Both Gabe and the doctor whirled and bolted into the examining room to see Polly hugging her dead husband and crying almost hysterically.

Gabe had seen his share of grief. He'd lost his mother, his wife, and his child in a raid by calvary on his Indian village. He'd seen squaws tear out their hair and slice themselves until they almost died of blood loss after the death of a child or a husband. He'd seen death come hard to Indian children with chicken pox and other white man's diseases and he'd killed men himself and known a hollow sickness in his gut.

Now he saw Polly in the depth of her grief and he stood as empty and helpless as if he had never seen grief before and did not know how to act. But then, did anyone ever learn how to comfort someone whose heart had just been broken? Gabe doubted it.

He and the doctor finally pried the widow from her husband after a time and took her outside. Gabe sat with Polly while the doctor made the funeral arrangements, and then they went out into the cold, gray afternoon and stood side by side without words.

When Polly began to shake with a chill, Gabe loaded her into her wagon. He drove it back to Oreville, to the shed behind Betsy's house, and quickly retrieved his horse and saddle. Then, he drove Polly back to the ranch and sat her before a big fire in her living room and made her drink hot coffee while he rubbed circulation back into her frozen hands and feet.

She never communicated the whole time, except through her eyes. Her eyes said everything. Her thanks and her sorrow and her sense of loss.

"Lay down and go to sleep," he said, "I'll be right here if you need me."

Polly nodded her head and closed her eyes. But it was a long, long time before sleep came and she finally breathed easily again.

CHAPTER SEVEN

Because the ground was frozen, it took two men a full day to get the grave dug. Gabe drove Polly to the cemetery, where they met the undertaker's hearse.

"There's a good-sized crowd today," the undertaker said, looking very pleased. He blew warm breath into his bony hands and ordered his assistants to pull the casket out. "Good-sized crowd, considering this awful weather."

Polly said nothing. There were about forty people, many of whom were Union Pacific folks who had worked with Chris. Others were clients that he had helped one way or the other.

"Your husband wasn't of our faith," a Mormon elder said. "But he was a very good and decent man. Whenever our own attorney was busy, Mr. Benton was our first choice."

"Thank you for saying that, Mr. Glass. Chris tried hard to be fair and honest with everyone he met."

Betsy came up to Polly. "I didn't know your husband, but Gabe has told me a lot about him and I wanted to express my condolences, Mrs. Benton. Gabe says your husband was honest and decent.''

Polly glanced at Long Rider and he could not read her expression. "Thank you, Miss Rogers," she said, turning back to the Oreville schoolteacher. "It was kind of you to come out in this weather."

The weather was nasty. The sky was pale blue and cloudless but there was a stiff wind blowing that cut through everyone. The undertaker's assistants quickly lowered the casket into the frozen ground, and then everyone turned to the preacher, who opened his Bible and seemed to consider it very carefully before he closed it again.

"Dear friends, it grieves me to see such a fine man as Mr. Benton put to rest this day. He was a friend to all, an enemy to none. Not even to those that he won victories over in court. I knew him very little, yet when we did meet, I could see that the hand of God was resting on his shoulder. He . . .''

Long Rider did not hear anymore because right then one of the horses in the team that had pulled the hearse jumped back and tried to run away. It would have succeeded with a little help from its partner. Gabe was the first to grab the horse's reins and he quieted the animal as the preacher droned on.

It seemed to Long Rider that the whites had a poor way of paying tribute to their dead. Words were hollow things, especially when given by a man who hardly knew the deceased. And even if it had been Gabe himself speaking, or Polly, the person closest to Chris, words would always be inadequate to express the value of a person's life.

Gabe thought it much better that those who most loved the deceased kept their memories locked inside like treasured things. It seemed to Long Rider that this eulogy business was a hollow performance. A ritual that had little warmth and even less sincerity.

". . . and so, my dear friends, be comforted in the mercy of God and know that Christian P. Benton rests in the cradle of heaven. Amen."

It was done and Gabe looked to Polly. As he had expected, she did not seem at all comforted. In fact, she looked more grief stricken than she had before the ceremony.

Gabe scowled. He watched strangers shovel dirt onto the casket and heard it land hollowly. Each shovelful caused Polly to wince as if being punched.

Gabe looked away. He was thoroughly disgusted and wished that they had buried Chris on the ranch, which he had so loved. But there had been a formal death certificate and the civil authorities had insisted that he be buried here.

This sure wasn't like the Plains Indians, who buried their dead on scaffolds with their most prized possessions. Up in the sky the spirit world was much closer to a dead warrior. Up in the sky a man's spirit was free to lift from his body slowly, like the rising of the sun, or it could soar quickly like an eagle on a column of wind.

But buried in the earth . . . that was wrong to Gabe's way of thinking. He would have to make sure that if he had any choice in the matter of his own death, his body would be placed up on the burial scaffold in the custom of the Indian.

Gabe waited until all the people had paid their respects to Polly and started to leave. One of the very last of them was the Ogden banker, Mr. Dalton Kimbal. Kimbal was a tall, gray-haired man in his early sixties. He wore tailored suits and was the most prominent banker in town. His Frontier Bank wasn't owned by the Mormon church, and everyone not of that faith, and some who were, did business there. Gabe had no money and therefore had never been interested in the banker. But he was now.

"Mr. Kimbal," he said after the man had expressed his condolences to Polly, "can I speak to you for a moment?"

"Of course, Gabe. I should have expressed my condolences to you as well. Even though you are uneducated and were raised among savages, I know that Chris thought the world of you. We share the burden of his death because we were both his very close friends."

Gabe bristled inwardly at the reference to "savages," but Chris had used his dying breath to ask him to speak with this man about the mortgage, and so he bit his tongue and swallowed the insult.

"We need to talk about the mortgage that is on the Benton ranch."

Kimbal raised his bushy eyebrows. "Is there some problem?"

"Chris thought so. How much is owed?"

Kimbal frowned. "Is this really the time or place to talk business?"

"How much is due every month?" Gabe asked, determined not to be swept aside. "I need to know that right now."

Kimbal pursed his lips. "I don't know the exact figures offhand. You see, I merely arranged the loan in the amount of twelve thousand dollars. I was also trying to raise money for the same mining venture and I simply did not have the funds to help Chris myself. We're a small bank and so I arranged for Chris to obtain the funds through a Salt Lake City bank called the Bank of Deseret."

"I understand that," Gabe said, pressed for an answer. "But you must have a pretty good idea."

"It's easy enough to figure because the mortgage is for twelve thousand dollars, payable over the next three years at nine percent. That means the monthly payment must be . . . oh, around three hundred eighty dollars a month."

Gabe almost fell over. "That much! No wonder Chris was worried."

"You have cattle and one of the best ranches in this territory. The property value warranted the size of the loan."

"The ranch can't make that much money. Not every single month."

Kimbal frowned. "What about cash?"

"I don't know," Gabe said. "But I doubt if he had much in savings. Chris was so young and successful, I think he figured he'd live another forty years and retire rich."

"He was heading down that road, all right. But a man never knows when his time has come to leave this earthly existence."

Gabe shook his head. "I'll come into town and we can talk later. I don't want to upset Polly with this for at least a few days."

Kimbal nodded. "If you sell the livestock, you've gutted the income production of the ranch. My advice would be to sell off that east section of the ranch. It's not good grazing land, anyway."

"But it's got all our timber and the water off Deer Creek."

"You could probably get enough money from the sale to pay off the mortgage to the Bank of Deseret and have enough left over to drill wells on the west section. Put in some water tanks. A lot of people in these parts do that without any problems. The water table is high out there."

Gabe knew that was true. "I don't know," he said. "Deer Creek runs year round. It's mighty important to the ranch."

"So is meeting that mortgage on time. I'm just suggesting it as a way to keep the ranch without liquidating the stock and eliminating your beef production. I'd like to see Mrs. Benton keep that ranch and not be forced to sell it at a loss. There are a lot of sharpsters who buy ranches that are facing foreclosure and they get them for ten cents on the dollar.''

''Well, couldn't you help out a little?''

''How? By loaning Mrs. Benton more money? Even though I have recovered sufficiently from those mining losses, it would be quite a burden. You see, I've just joined our bank with a bank in Reno. That has been expensive but now there are *two* Frontier Banks, and we hope that someday there will be dozens helping folks across the West.''

''Well, maybe those people in Reno could help out a little.''

''I'm sure they could. There's Comstock money in our Reno branch. Their deposits dwarf ours here in Ogden.''

''Mr. Kimbal, give the idea some thought,'' Gabe said. ''I think you know that our eastern part of the ranch is worth plenty, given the amount of timber and water.''

''That's true, but I'm no rancher.''

''I understand,'' Gabe said. ''But you were a friend of Chris and you'd sure be helping out his widow.''

''I'll think about it,'' Kimbal promised. ''I would have to send a telegram to the folks in Reno about this. . . .''

''Why don't you do that?'' Gabe said. ''There's not much chance of coming up with a buyer other than yourself. Not for a fair price.''

''All right,'' Kimbal said, ''I will.''

Gabe felt a tremendous sense of relief. ''The decision, of course, will be Polly's, but at least when I tell her about it, she'll have an option.''

''I understand completely. Any idea what she will ask for that part of the ranch?''

''No,'' Gabe admitted. ''But it will be fair. Polly will

understand what you're trying to do to help us. We just have to get her out from under the Bank of Deseret.''

''Of course.''

The banker shook Gabe's rough hand. ''Again, my deepest, most heartfelt condolences to both you and Mrs. Benton.''

''Thanks,'' Gabe said as he turned and waited to take Polly back to the ranch.

It was not until they had gotten back in the buggy and were ready to go that Polly remarked, ''What did you and Mr. Kimbal have to talk so much about?''

''Nothin' important,'' Gabe said as he took up the lines and got the buggy moving down the road.

Polly twisted around and took a farewell look at the cemetery before she turned back to Gabe. ''Don't try to hide things from me, Gabe. I'm not a little girl that will fall apart. I need to know what you talked about, since you are not a depositor in that man's bank.''

''Chris didn't want me to tell you, but I guess I have no choice. The truth is, there's a twelve-thousand-dollar mortgage due on your ranch and monthly payments we can't meet. The mortgage is held by the Bank of Deseret in Salt Lake City.''

''But Chris never told me about that!''

''I guess he was ashamed to admit that he lost so much money in a mining venture that he and Mr. Kimbal were heavily invested in.''

Polly expelled a deep breath. ''Chris was a wonderful attorney and a fine man, but he was terrible at investments. Before we met he invested in another mining venture and lost everything. I had thought he'd learned a hard lesson.''

''Polly, before he died, your welfare was all he could. think of.''

The woman was silent for a long time before she said,

"We'll just have to figure out something. That ranch was a part of Chris. I see him . . . and you, in every corral and barn that you both put up. If it hadn't been for his law practice here in town, we'd have lived there on a permanent basis. And now that he's gone, that's what I'll do. We'll find a way together."

"I think we might already have something figured out with Mr. Kimbal." In as much detail as he could, Gabe explained how the Ogden banker had agreed to query his counterpart in Reno about buying a part of the ranch.

"It's a solution, but not one that I relish," she said when he was finished. "That eastern part up near the mountains is the most beautiful part of our ranch."

"Beauty won't pay off the mortgage," Gabe argued. "And we can drill wells. Sometimes streams dry up during bad years, but wells generally do not."

"All right, then," Polly said. "If Mr. Kimbal can help us get a fair price, enough to pay off the Bank of Deseret and have some left to drill those wells, then I'll do it."

"Good," he said. "In a few days, we'll go back to Ogden and see if the Reno people are going to okay the loan."

CHAPTER EIGHT

They had arrived back at the ranch late that night, and for the next few days, Gabe had his hands full taking care of cattle and horses. It had stopped snowing but it was bitterly cold, and that meant the livestock had to eat more just to stay even in their weight.

Diablo had refused to eat the first couple of days but then had apparently decided he wanted to live and was now eating everything Gabe tossed into the breaking corral. The stallion had lost a good hundred pounds since they'd captured him up in the Bear River country. He was coated with mud and his eyes rolled and he snorted whenever Gabe opened the gate.

The first time Gabe had stepped in to look at the Appaloosa, his hand had slipped to the gun at his side when he thought about what this horse had done to Chris. But Gabe had backed away knowing it was wrong to blame the wild stallion. At that moment, he decided that his best revenge would be to conquer the animal by riding it to a standstill for Chris's sake, and then he'd feel good about turning Diablo loose.

On the morning that Gabe finally caught up with his work and decided to ride Diablo, Polly said, "Let's go to Ogden to talk to Mr. Kimbal today."

"I don't think there's any hurry. Maybe you ought to rest for a few more days and then we can go."

"No," she said decisively. "I'll just keep worrying about that mortgage until we find out if the Frontier Bank can pay if off. Did Mr. Kimbal know when the next payment was due?"

"I forgot to ask."

"Well, see? It might be due tomorrow, and then we'll have penalties to pay on top of everything else. I want to get the matter settled now."

"All right."

Gabe hitched the team back up and they returned to Ogden. When they walked into the Frontier Bank, Mr. Kimbal did not seem especially surprised to see them.

"Sit, both of you," he said, looking at Polly. "Mrs. Benton, this really could wait if you don't feel up to it."

"No, it's like I told Gabe. I want to settle this thing and I've been thinking about your suggestion regarding the sale of our eastern two thousand acres of watershed and timber. It's the finest and most valuable land we own."

"I know that," the bank said. "But as I pointed out to Gabe, it's not of value to your cattle. In fact, when I was young and helped the man who owned the ranch previously on his spring roundups, that eastern part was a real liability. It had so much timber and rocky ground it made snaking the cattle out a real chore. It ought to be fenced off. I'd fence it off if it were mine."

"Do you want it to be yours?" Gabe asked bluntly.

Kimbal steepled his fingers. They were long and the nails were manicured. They were pretty hands that had never held a shovel or an ax or a plow. "I might have to buy it."

"What do you mean?" Polly asked suddenly.

Kimbal shook his head. "I'm afraid our Reno bank has turned the suggestion down cold. They don't know this country and they were just afraid that it would be an unsound investment."

It was a hard blow for Polly, and Gabe steeled himself. "Do you have the money to buy it yourself?"

"If the price is right, I believe I might be able to swing the deal. How much do you think that property is worth to you, Mrs. Benton?"

Polly replied, "As you know, my back is to the wall."

"I wouldn't make an offer that I didn't think was fair. I am not in business to take advantage of my friends and depositors, Mrs. Benton. I do need to hear a price."

Polly had obviously been giving it some thought. "If a person logged in there, they could realize a nice income. Also, Chris always felt that there was a strong possibility that gold and silver might be found up by the canyons."

"Please, just give me a figure. I know the land."

"Why would a man like you want it?" Gabe asked.

"Three reasons. First, I spent some time hunting and fishing there as a boy. Second, if I keep it long enough, I can show a profit on it and show those folks in Reno that they were wrong to turn us down now. And third, I am aware of no other buyer who would take the property, which means I might have to watch the ranch slip away from Mrs. Benton. That would not bring joy to this banker's heart."

Gabe nodded and looked at Polly. It was up to her to state a figure. Gabe had his own idea what the property was worth—about fourteen thousand dollars—but he had not been asked and he would not volunteer that information unless he was asked.

"Fifteen thousand," she said, looking Kimbal right in the eye. "That would give me enough money to pay off your bank and also to drill those water wells that you talked to Gabe about. Plus, I'd have a little extra for emergencies."

Dalton Kimbal studied his immaculate hands for a long while and then he looked up and smiled. "Very well, fifteen thousand it is. I will write out a bill of sale, you can come back in an hour, and it will be notarized and the money credited to your account. I'll give you a draft for twelve thousand, which you can take to the Bank of Deseret and pay off that mortgage. I'll just leave the other three thousand here on deposit, earning you interest."

"That will be fine. I wouldn't think of taking it to another bank. I'm very grateful," Polly said.

"And I'm just happy I can help you this way," Kimbal said. "And so now, if you will leave me be for an hour, I'll have everything ready to sign when you return."

They left the bank and walked over to the Outrider Cafe, where they ate quietly. Gabe kept glancing up at Polly and was pleased to discover that she looked better. The dark circles were still under her eyes, but there was no longer a tight, strained look.

"You seem happy about the deal," he said when they were finished eating and a second cup of coffee had been poured.

"Oh, I am! I'm rather shocked that Mr. Kimbal agreed to my price. I thought certain that he would counter my offer and we'd settle at the amount of the mortgage he holds. I feel very, very fortunate."

"He's a generous man. He wanted to help."

"What surprises me most," Polly said, "is that Chris always told me that when it came to money Dalton Kimbal had no friends. Chris said he was in the business strictly to make money for himself."

"Then I guess that piece of property really did hold a sentimental attachment for him," Gabe said, signaling the waitress that he wanted a piece of apple pie. "That, and it sounds like he really wants to show those people at the other Frontier Bank in Reno that they were wrong."

"I guess," Polly said. "But for whatever reason, I am sincerely grateful to the man. I can't tell you what a burden this takes off my shoulders. Chris loved that ranch so much that I feel an obligation to somehow keep it. And I'll need your help."

"I know that," Gabe said, digging into his pie and finding it very much to his satisfaction.

They talked awhile longer and when the hour was up, they returned to the Frontier Bank and all the papers were in order just as promised.

"You'll notice," Kimbal said, "that I've dated that twelve-thousand-dollar check for next Monday. That will give me an extra day or two to muster my finances in order to cover the check."

Polly's eyes widened with immediate alarm. "Do you mean there could be a problem?"

"Of course not. I just have to transfer the necessary funds. It will give me a little more breathing room. You take that check to the Bank of Deseret and they will clear the funds by Wednesday through our bank and you'll have that canceled mortgage from them the very same afternoon."

"Thank you so much," Polly said, carefully folding the check and putting it into her purse. "I can't imagine how Chris ever allowed himself to get mixed up in that mining-stock venture that caused all this trouble."

"The fourth reason I'm doing this and the one I did not mention, is that I'm partly to blame for that," Kimbal admitted. "I suffered far more severe losses than your late husband."

"I'm sorry to hear that," Polly said. "But seeing as how you just bought a sizable part of my ranch, you must have recovered rather nicely."

"I word hard at it," Kimbal said. "Besides, that timber on your ranch is a long-term investment. And unlike gold or silver, I *know* it's there for the eventual taking. By the way, your three thousand dollars will be earning six-percent interest from this very moment."

Polly raised her eyebrows. "I thought it would be nine."

"Oh no! Nine is what we loan money at. The difference between the lending and the borrowing rate is our profit."

"I see," Polly said. "No wonder your Frontier Banks are doing such a good business."

Kimbal shrugged. "All banks charge about the same. Good day, Mrs. Benton. Nice doing business with you."

When they climbed back in the buggy and headed for home, Polly said, "I thank God that there are men like Dalton Kimbal who put their hearts into banking instead of just their hands. He has really done us a favor."

"That's for sure."

"Though I am going to deeply regret not owning that timber and water."

"We'll raise a lot of beef. Who knows?" Long Rider said. "Maybe someday you can buy it back."

Polly looked at him closely. "Maybe we can buy it back together."

Gabe said nothing as he drove on. Polly Benton was a beautiful woman and one he'd always secretly admired. But the painful memory of Chris was a thing that stood between them too strongly right now. And maybe it always would.

CHAPTER NINE

Polly was upset with Long Rider as he gathered a bridle and an old bucking saddle, a rope, and a blindfold.

"This is crazy! Why risk your neck trying to ride a killer that you intend to turn loose?"

"It's just something I have to do . . . for Chris . . . and for myself," he said, avoiding her accusing eyes. "I didn't expect you to understand."

"You're darned right I don't understand! That horse could kill you!"

Gabe said nothing as he carried his gear toward the breaking corral. He could see Diablo through the cracks in the fence, and the animal was pacing back and forth, just as it always did.

"Isn't there anything I can do or say to change your mind?"

"You can fire me and tell me to get off the property. Diablo belonged to Chris so he belongs to you now."

"Then I'll turn him loose!"

Polly swept around him and ran to the gate. She opened

it and turned to look at Gabe, who was regarding her without any emotion. Polly stamped her food down hard. "Say something!"

"I've said my piece," he told her. "We both have to do what we have to do."

Polly slammed the gate shut again. "Dammit, but you make me angry. If I turn the stallion loose, you'll hate me."

"No, I won't."

"But you won't like me as much. There'd be a wedge driven between us that wouldn't go away."

Gabe just stood waiting, the saddle hanging at his side along with the blanket and other gear he would need to ride Diablo. He knew Polly well enough to understand that she would talk herself out of this corner and then she'd be fine.

"All right! You win, but I'm getting a Winchester and stuffing the barrel through the fence, and I'll shoot that stallion if he gets you down."

"If that's what you've got to do," Gabe said, moving past the woman, who raced toward the house to get a rifle.

Gabe turned all his attention on the stallion. Even gaunt and caked with mud, he was still a great-looking horse. Right now, though, he had his ears back and looked as if he were about ready to attack.

Gabe dropped his saddle and bridle and made a tight loop with his rope. There was a log snubbing post in the exact center of the corral and it was as big around as a man's thigh and set four feet deep in the ground. Now, he was betting it would save his life.

Diablo pawed the damp earth. He snorted and shook his head. He remembered that Gabe had been the man with the rope who had caught him in his box canyon hideout up in the Bear River country.

"Come on and let's start the dance," Gabe said quietly,

his feet set square and the loop hanging ready to be flicked upward the moment the stallion made his rush.

Diablo squealed and charged. He was quicker than a cat and Gabe threw right at his face, then dived sideways, rolled, and sprinted for the snubbing post. He got two fast wraps around the post before Diablo could reverse his direction and come back after him. Gabe took up the slack as he raced to the wall of the pen, and then whirled and dug in his heels.

Diablo hit the end of the rope and went crazy when the noose tightened about his throat. He reared up and fought the rope and then he lunged. The noose tightened about his throat even more and he went down thrashing and choking for air as Gabe jumped forward with a blindfold.

It was over in a very few seconds. Gabe had won again and he had Diablo blindfolded and hobbled before he loosened the noose and gave the animal some air to breathe. He retrieved his saddle and bridle and in less than five minutes, he was ready to cut the hobbles and make his ride.

"I'll shoot him if you go down!" Polly yelled.

Gabe turned to see a rifle barrel poking through the fence. "You're about as likely to shoot me as this horse. So don't get trigger happy."

Not waiting for an answer, Gabe threw a leg over the saddle and then he cut the hobble. Diablo surged to his feet and the moment he was up, Gabe yanked the blindfold away.

The Appaloosa stallion went crazy. It shot straight up into the air and came down stiff legged, pile-driving Gabe and snapping his chin down against his chest. Diablo erupted skyward a second time, swapping ends and screeching like a wounded wildcat. He sunfished and reared, bucked, and did more brutal pile drives as Gabe hung on with all his strength.

Diablo squealed in frustration at the man who would not be shaken loose. He threw himself at the snubbing post in a demented attempt to rake Gabe from his back. Gabe had to pull his boot out of the stirrup or his leg would have been crushed. As it was, the stirrup was torn loose and the heavy post splintered.

"Gabe, get off him!" Polly shouted.

Gabe had the same idea. There was no way that he could ride this horse with only one stirrup. Any moment now he would be hurled into the fence and probably knocked unconscious. Diablo would stomp him before Polly could get enough killing rounds into the animal to bring him down.

Gabe attempted to time his jump for the fence and he must have done a fair job because when he launched himself out of the saddle he was thrown right over the fence. Everything would have been fine if he hadn't caught his pant leg on the top of the fence and hung suspended upside down for a moment, half-in and half-out of the corral.

Diablo saw him and made a lunge with his big teeth ready to sink into Gabe's leg. Polly fired but the bullet missed, and then Gabe's pant leg tore free and he crashed outside the breaking corral, landing hard on his left shoulder.

"Gabe!" Polly cried, racing to his side. "Are you all right?"

He wasn't all right. He managed to sit up but there was so much pain in his shoulder that he could not lift his arm.

"I'll get him next time," Gabe said, allowing Polly to help him to his feet.

"There won't be a next time," she vowed as she helped him to the ranch house, where she removed his shirt and examined his arm.

"It isn't broken, is it?"

"I don't know," she said. "But if it isn't, then it's a terrible bruise. It might also be dislocated."

"It will mend," Gabe said. "I've been hurt plenty worse."

Polly looked ready to kill him. "Well, that's not exactly comforting! I can tell by all these scars you wear that you've been shot, beat up by soldiers, knifed, and God knows what else."

"Pistol-whipped," he said. "Just recently, as a matter of fact."

"Yes, that, too. We're going to go into Ogden and see the doctor about this shoulder."

"No," Gabe said. "I got work to do here yet."

"I'm telling you we are leaving right now."

Gabe decided not to argue. He was tired of arguing, and beside, his shoulder felt like it was being jabbed by fiery needles. The pain was so intense that he wanted to bite a stick, and he could feel a numbness in his left hand.

"I'll get the buggy hitched," Polly said. "We can stay in town through Monday and then we'll get the loan and that mortgage business taken care of while you recover."

"I can recover just about as well right here."

"Well, I've still got some recovering to do myself and I want to do it in town," Polly told him.

Gabe remembered little about the ride into Ogden because he was awash in a sea of pain. When Polly led him into Dr. Wheeler's office, the physician took one look at his face and knew he was in agony.

"Take that buffalo coat off," he said.

Gabe did as he was told. Polly hadn't even bothered to try and put his shirt back on after her examination.

"It's a dislocation," the doctor said after he made his own unhurried examination. "I can tell by the way that left clavicle bone is protruding all out of line. That, and you've torn some muscle tissue. What happened to you this time?''

"I'd rather not talk about it," Gabe said.

"Of course he wouldn't!" Polly said angrily. "The fool tried to ride Diablo. Tried to ride him after that same horse killed my husband."

Doc Wheeler looked Gabe in the eye. "You *are* a fool to do that," he said quietly. "You're probably lucky to be alive."

Gabe said nothing. He was not a man to argue or make excuses, and he was as stubborn as Chris when it came to carrying out his intentions. He'd rest and recover, all right, but he'd also go back and ride Diablo or die trying. Only next time, he'd do it when Polly wasn't around and he'd be ready when Diablo tried to smash his leg into the snubbing post.

"I'm going to have to put this shoulder in a sling," the doctor said. "It needs to be immobilized."

"How long will I have to use the sling?"

"I can't say, exactly. A week or two," the doctor said, fashioning a sling and adjusting it so Gabe's arm hung across his chest and his hand was resting just below his heart.

Gabe stood up feeling hurt and angry. "After we get the banking stuff done and the mortgage paid off next Wednesday, I've got to get back to work. The stock doesn't care if I'm hurt or not. They'll be hungry."

Polly nodded. "We'll just play it a day at a time, bronc rider."

Gabe's cheeks colored. Polly was pulling his leg.

On Monday morning, Polly and Gabe had a leisurely breakfast and were just leaving for Salt Lake City when they saw a small crowd gathered at the Frontier Bank.

"It's a few minutes after ten o'clock," Polly said. "Why do you suppose the bank isn't open yet?"

"Beats me," Gabe said. "Maybe Mr. Kimbal overslept."

"Until after ten o'clock? That doesn't seem possible."

Gabe shrugged. He had already hitched up their buggy and was ready to roll. They'd stop at the Bank of Deseret and pay off their mortgage, then be back at the ranch before dark if they moved along smartly.

They were starting to walk on when suddenly a man came running up to the crowd and yelled, "Mr. Kimbal is gone! The liveryman said he got his horse last night and took a pack animal with him. Said it was after midnight and Mr. Kimbal looked mighty grim."

Polly froze. "You don't think . . . ."

"I don't know," Gabe said. "But we'd better find out."

They both hurried over to the bank and Gabe said, "Has anyone thought to pay a visit to the man's house?"

"What for?" an anxious depositor cried. "We know he left Ogden last night."

"But why?" Gabe asked. "That's the big question."

"Well, he lives just two blocks over on Second Street."

Gabe and Polly started off in that direction and a gathering crowd followed them. When they came to the banker's door, Gabe did not bother to knock.

"It's unlocked," he said, turning the door handle.

They went inside. It was a big house and would have been impressive if it were not for the fact that the rooms were empty, except for the drapes. They moved from room to room, their shoes echoing on the hardwood floors.

Upstairs in the bedrooms, it was the same story. Empty, everything empty.

Polly turned to the anxious crowd. "How long has it been since anyone has visited Mr. Kimbal?"

No one could say. Finally, a man cleared his throat.

"Mr. Kimbal has been a loner since that mining venture he and your husband were in failed a couple of years ago."

Polly looked at Gabe and put into words his exact thoughts. "He sold or shipped everything he owned and then he ran."

Gabe nodded and both of them were thinking that they had better get inside the Frontier Bank and see if they could get ahold of Polly's three thousand dollars on deposit before there was a rush on the bank.

They hurried outside and down the street to the bank. By now, word of Mr. Kimbal's disappearance had spread all over Ogden and there was a large crowd gathering in front of the bank. Gabe kicked in the front door and everyone surged into the lobby and they froze in their tracks.

The vault door was hanging wide open.

Gabe felt a deep sense of dread forming in the pit of his stomach. He rushed across the lobby and when he reached the vault, he stuck his head through the open doorway.

"Empty," he said. "Cleaned out."

As a result of that pronouncement, everyone began to shout and curse all at once. Men started to ransack the drawers and the counter shelves as if their deposits might have been overlooked by Kimbal.

"Come on," Gabe said. "We've got a check for twelve thousand dollars drawn on this bank and we'd better get to the Bank of Deseret and trade it for that mortgage or we're in deep trouble."

Polly did not have to be told twice. They hurried outside and ran to their buggy. By now, the entire town was milling around in the street and it looked to Gabe as if there was going to be a riot in Ogden.

"I never thought he'd do something like this!" Polly exclaimed as Gabe whipped the team down the street and careened around the last corner of the thoroughfare as he lined the buggy out for Salt Lake City. "I never liked the man but he seemed so honest and sincere in wanting to help us and to own that eastern section of our ranch.''

"He was probably honest until things went bad for him. Only instead of working his way out of debt, he decided to wait for the right moment and then abscond with tens, perhaps even hundreds of thousand of dollars.''

"He'll break this town!'' Polly cried. "The Frontier Bank was the biggest and most popular non-Mormon bank in Ogden. People like me will lose everything.''

Gabe heard the sound of racing hooves behind them and then he turned around as three riders overtook and went charging past them.

"We're lost,'' he said, whipping the team as fast as it would run but still falling farther and farther behind. "They'll spread the word before we can get that mortgage from the Bank of Deseret. That twelve-thousand-dollar check Kimbal wrote out to you won't be worth the paper that it's printed on.''

"Then I'll lose the ranch!''

Gabe pulled the buggy in to a dusty standstill. "Is the telegraph line to Reno still out?''

"Why, yes. The Paiutes are on the warpath to the west of us. They've been burning Nevada outposts and . . . What are you thinking of, Gabe?''

"I'm thinking that Kimbal said there were *two* Frontier Bank branches. And if we can reach the one in Reno before it hears about this, we've still got a chance to cash that check.''

Polly's eyes widened. "Yes! You're right! But it's better than five hundred miles to Reno! And those Indians.''

"It's our only hope,'' Gabe said. "We either beat the next westbound Pacific to Reno, or you've lost everything.''

"The westbound will be coming through in five days;

it will be in Reno two days later. It would be impossible to beat.''

"Not with the right horses under us,'' he said. "My sorrel gelding under you and me riding Diablo. They might just do it together.''

"You're out of your mind!''

"Am I?''

Polly took a deep breath and expelled it slowly. "How can you possibly ride that Appaloosa stallion with a bad shoulder!''

"All I have to do is ride him once to a standstill,'' Gabe said with determination. "I can teach that stallion the finer points of being a saddle horse as we race across the desert.''

Polly nodded. "Then let's try it.''

Gabe turned the team of buggy horses around and made them run. As bad as things were right now, he could not help but feel a rush of excitement. This was going to be a brutal horse race, and if they were very lucky, they just might pull it off and get Polly her twelve thousand dollars.

Long Rider tore off his sling and used his right hand to help lift his left up to a rail sitting at eye level. Grabbing the rail hard, he fought through the pain and leaned back until he felt the shoulder socket grate and then pop back into place. The effort left him weak and shaky.

He waited for several minutes until his mind cleared of the pain, and then he went for his gear. This time, he was going to ride Diablo or die trying.

Surprisingly, the Appaloosa stallion did not charge him again and he roped the horse and even managed to get it blindfolded and saddled without any real difficulty. Today, he had chosen to wear tight leather chaps and before he entered the corral, he squatted in the water trough. Maybe it was cheating a little, but he didn't give a damn. The wet chaps would adhere to the saddle leather and give him an edge. And with his bad arm, he needed some advantage.

Gabe placed his hand on the Appaloosa's heavily muscled shoulder. The animal was trembling but Gabe had the feeling it was not due to fear, but to anticipation.

Gabe looked over at Polly, who had taken a firing position near the gate. "Don't do it," he said. "Not unless I'm down and not moving. We need this animal. Without him, there's not a horse on the ranch that has the strength and toughness to carry me to Reno fast enough."

In answer, Polly levered a shell into the chamber of the Winchester. "If it's your life or the ranch, I'll shoot when I have to."

Gabe knew it was useless to argue further. He pulled his Stetson down tight and jammed his boot into the stirrup. Diablo was waiting.

The instant Gabe's right toe punched through his stirrup, the stallion launched himself skyward like a Chinese rocket. He came down stiff legged again, and Gabe's chin snapped down hard against his chest. Two more high jumps ended the same way and Gabe's nose began to bleed heavily. Every time the stallion went up, Gabe's neck snapped like a whip, and when Diablo began to sunfish, Gabe held on, riding out of instinct.

Man and horse fought each other without reason or thought. They just acted and reacted, each punishing the other—the horse with its terrible landings and wild twists that kept Gabe off balance, the man with the spurs.

Dimly, Gabe could hear Polly yelling encouragement but her voice was distant and it came to him in snatches as the world spun and jolted. He could also hear his own breath, and the taste of blood on his tongue was salty. Each time he landed, his bad shoulder felt as if someone had driven a spike straight to the core of his bone.

But ever so gradually, the feeling that he was riding with

desperation and would any moment be launched into the fence gave way to a feeling that he was slowly winning. He could hear the stallion's tortured breath above his own and he realized that the animal was nearing the point of collapse from its struggle.

The stallion's own difficulties gave Gabe hope. His vision seemed to focus and he raked the horse with his spurs every time it bucked until he could sense that Diablo was beaten. The Appaloosa was starting to run and buck now and all Gabe had to do was to pull its head up and keep it moving forward.

"You did it!" Polly cried.

Gabe sleeved away the mask of blood that covered the lower half of his face. He pulled the stallion's head up short to a standstill. Reaching down, he patted the big horse on the neck and said, "I need your strength and your heart. But I swear this, when the need is over, I will set you free."

Diablo, whose coat was dripping with sweat, shook his proud head. His nostrils were distended and his flanks were bloodied from the spurs. Even so, Gabe could feel the animal's raw power between his legs. He would grain the horse and then they would ride out within the hour.

To Reno, across five hundred miles of Paiute-infested desert hell.

CHAPTER TEN

The drab hotel room was chilly as Dalton Kimbal studied the two outlaws across from him with unconcealed suspicion and disgust. "All right," the banker said. "You've gotten me to Elko without anyone knowing it, but it's still a long way to Reno before you're going to get paid off."

Dan Barling was tall, broad-shouldered, and had an unnerving way of looking through a man. He was said to be ox strong and expert with a knife. Dan wore the scars of a dozen knife fights on his face and body.

His partner, Curly Cutter, was a fast-talking dandy who wore his gun low on his narrow hip with the front sight shaved off for a quicker draw. Curly was mouthy and a braggart. "Kimbal," he said, "we been thinking we need a little advance on our pay right now."

"Not a chance," the banker said, getting up and moving away from the pair. He had a derringer in his vest pocket, but he knew that he'd never live to get the damn thing in action if he tried to gun them down. Besides, he still needed them.

Relaxing, he forced a smile. "Listen, boys, I know it's against your nature to sit still and lie low, but that's what you'll have to do until the train comes through and we board for Reno."

"That's the better part of a week!" Curly complained. "Damned if I'm going to sit around here looking at the pair of you 'til then. The problem is, we're dead broke. Can't have any fun when you're broke, Mr. Kimbal."

"You're not here to have fun, damn you!"

Kimbal lowered his voice when he saw Curly's handsome face darken with fury. The banker knew he had gone too far. "Listen," he said in a conciliatory tone, "you men have to understand that you're both here to guard my life and to keep anyone from seeing me. I thought I made that very clear before I let you in on this."

"Well, you did," Barling said, "but we got you out of Ogden without a hitch and we made a damned hard ride over here to Elko. Seems to us, we've earned a little reward right now. Nothin' much, mind you, but a hundred dollars would buy us a little woman company and a few drinks."

"It would also likely buy you big trouble," Kimbal said. "If you get drunk and raise hell, you're going to get in a fight, and that means you'll either kill someone or get yourselves hanged, or else you'll have to clear out of town on the run—then where am I?"

The two men exchanged glances, then Dan Barling scratched his lantern jaw and drawled, "We both been run out of a lot of towns, but not one where we was guarding a man that was going to pay us a thousand dollars each. That's more money than we'd make in a year. I reckon we'd use good sense if you gave us some money and a little slack."

Kimbal realized that he could not force the two men to stay in this cramped hotel room. If they were determined to come and go, at least he could seem to give them permission and retain some measure of control. "If I give you enough money to go out and eat and have a few beers, then come back, will that satisfy you?"

"Not by half," Curly said, sticking his jaw out a little in defiance. He was fair complected with reddish blond hair and green eyes. He looked like a choirboy, but he was as deadly as a Mexican scorpion. "Mr. Kimbal, we are men, don't you know? And we ain't either of us had a woman in most near two weeks now. Wasn't any whores in Ogden and we ain't seen any squaws doing it for free. No, sir!"

Barling nodded. "There's a couple of places over on the back street. Maybe you'd like to come along?"

Kimbal almost lost his temper and his cheeks colored with his outrage. "Now that would be real smart, wouldn't it! And sure enough, someone would recognize me, and even though the telegraph is down, they'd start asking questions and wondering why a banker is hiding out."

Cutter clucked his tongue and frowned a moment before he said, "I got it! We'll hire a gal and bring her up here! That way, we could all take turns and not even have to go anywhere."

"No," Kimbal said, slamming his fist down on the table. "It would just be another complication. Besides, I don't want to be seen by anyone. How clear do I have to spell that out before you'll understand?"

Barling shifted his considerable weight on his feet. He was a restless man and from the looks of him, a natural athlete. If it wasn't for the terrible knife scars, he'd have been a catalog model for an eastern mail-order house.

"I guess you checked in a lot of money at that vault over at the Union Pacific railway office. Probably got a bunch more in that valise over there by your bed."

Kimbal's mouth went dry. "What I have in there are

securities and notes that are redeemable only at the Frontier Bank in Reno.''

Cutter chuckled. ''Sure they are! I'll bet what you got is cold cash!''

Kimbal felt a chill pass through his body but he tried not to show his alarm. ''Just you both start worrying about keeping up your end of the deal and not about things that don't concern you.''

''Money concerns us,'' Barling said. ''It concerns anyone with any sense.''

''All right,'' Kimbal said in a rush, as he pulled out his wallet. ''Here's fifty dollars. But it's got to last you right up until the train comes through and we're on board. Is that understood?''

The pair grinned and nodded. ''Course, if we was to bring you up a real pretty lady . . .''

''I don't want a woman, dammit!'' Kimbal raged. ''All I want is to be protected until that train arrives. And if you hear of anybody asking questions about me, I want to know that, too.''

''You want us to shut them up permanent?''

''No!'' the banker squawked. ''But there's bound to be people looking for me. Your job is to make sure they don't find me. If you fail at that, you'll get nothing.''

Barling stuck out his hand. ''How about the fifty dollars?''

Kimbal was careful not to let them peek into his wallet. He was carrying too much cash, even though it was nothing compared to the value of the checks he had deposited in the railway office for safekeeping all the way to Reno.

''Here,'' he crabbed, extending the money.

Cutter snatched the fifty dollars away. With the cash in his fist, he grew excessively cocky. ''Say now, Mr. Kimbal, don't you worry about a damn thing. We'll be back before too long.''

"You'd better be."

Cutter chuckled to himself and headed for the door. He went out without a backward glance but Barling paused at the door. "You know what I think, Mr. Kimbal?"

"I don't care what you think."

Barling acted as if he hadn't heard him. "Mr. Kimbal," he said, his eyes squinting, "back in Ogden, there's probably a lot of folks who'd pay a handsome reward for your capture and return."

Kimbal swallowed. He forced himself not to break eye contact with the man. "Don't think and you'll do a lot better for yourself," he said in a voice that sounded stretched and too high. "I'm paying you well. And if you must think, do it about the money you'll make in Reno instead of what may or may not be offered back in Ogden."

"I have been," Barling confessed. "It's just that a thousand dollars don't quite seem so much the more as Curly and I think about it. I mean, it's nothing compared to what you stole from those folks back in Ogden."

"Get out of here and behave yourselves!" Kimbal hissed.

Barling smiled. One of his knife scars had cut through his lips so that his grin was twisted and diabolical looking. Kimbal felt his heart pound as the door closed and he was alone.

"I've got to get rid of them," he said to himself out loud when he was alone. "The bastards are going to double-cross me the first good chance they have to get my money."

Kimbal began to pace the floor. He had needed the pair of cutthroats to help him get out of Utah and he still needed them to protect him in case anyone from Ogden might happen to come into this town. But once he was on the westbound train, maybe then he could eliminate the pair.

That way, he'd not only be saving his own neck, but also saving himself a little money.

But how could he kill them before they killed him? Killing, after all, was *their* business, not his. He was a banker. Would still be a banker if it hadn't been for some very disastrous mining investments with money that had not been authorized for his use.

Dalton Kimbal went to his window and saw the two men emerge in the street below. They were moving toward a saloon and he heard their harsh laughter. Curly turned just before entering the saloon and looked up and across the street straight at Kimbal, who froze beside his window curtains. For a moment their eyes locked, and then Curly laughed again and made an obscene gesture with his hips.

Shocked and humiliated, Kimbal retreated from the window and cursed the man, vowing to find a way to kill him and Barling on the way to Reno. He went to his valise and opened it to look at the money he was carrying.

Two thousand dollars. It wasn't much. Not seven percent of what he'd deposited in the vault over at the railroad station and insured. That was the real prize. The money that Cutter and Barling were hoping to get once they arrived in Reno.

If I can't outgun them, then I'll poison them on the train, Kimbal thought.

He considered the idea from every angle. He could sprinkle their food or drink with some lethal poison and avoid all suspicion if it was done correctly. Yes, that would be the best way. They would never suspect him of doing them in like that. Poison was a woman's way of murder.

So break the rules, Kimbal thought. All that really counts is who lives to walk into the Frontier Bank of Reno with a stack of checks to cash on demand. Add that money to what he now was staring at and what also rested in the railroad office vault, and you had a nice, tidy fortune.

Enough money to live out the rest of your natural life in high style.

The banker caressed the money in his valise. The touch of it brought him great and immediate comfort, just as it always had.

Standing up, Kimbal hurried back over to his window. There was a general store still open down the street. In it, he would find rat poison and maybe even something stronger used for poisoning coyotes or wolves. Wolves. Curly Cutter and Dan Barling were nothing but human wolves in need of killing.

Dalton Kimbal locked his valise and shoved it under his bed. He might not have another chance at getting the poison so he had to act right now.

He used his key to lock the hotel room door and then hurried off down the threadbare hallway. He had never killed men before, only cheated or robbed them of their money. But it seemed that once a man stepped across a line, anything was possible and nothing was so reprehensible. Besides, this was a matter of survival. If Cutter and Barling were honorable men with honorable intentions, then none of this poisoning business would be necessary.

Kimbal checked the derringer in his vest pocket and moved cautiously down the backstairs into the alley. His heart was pounding and he tried to remind himself that it was highly unlikely that anyone from Ogden would be looking for him in Elko so soon. After all, there was a Paiute Indian war, and even though most of the trouble was taking place farther west in the central part of Nevada, the uprising would discourage pursuit from Utah. Kimbal and his two companions had ridden hard and at night to avoid any trouble and had considered themselves very fortunate not to have met any Indians.

The banker emerged from the alley and straightened his derby hat, then lifted his chin and tried to look as casual as possible as he strolled down the boardwalk toward the general store. Even so, several men gave him hard and, he thought, curious looks.

"Good day," Kimbal said to a pair of cowboys who blocked his path on the boardwalk.

The cowboys nodded and stepped aside for him, and he continued on toward the store, certain that someone from Ogden was about to put a bullet through his breast.

"Evening!" the owner of the general store said in greeting. "I was just about to close up for the night, but I'm happy to stay for business. What can I do for you?"

"Uh . . . I could use a new razor," he stammered, suddenly realizing how suspicious it would appear if he only asked for poison. "And . . . oh, yes, some rat poison."

The proprietor, a short, balding man in his fifties, chuckled sympathetically. "Yeah, I been having rat problems myself. Damn things have taken over my hay barn. They're getting so big that they've got my tomcat buffaloed!"

"Oh," Kimbal said in an absent voice. "I suppose they can become quite vicious."

"Well, step over here and I'll show you what we have. It's the best poison on the market. Here, just read what it says on the box."

Kimbal did not care what it said on the box, but he forced himself to read it anyway. Doc Potter's Rat Killer was made out of a substance call strychnine, a colorless, tasteless crystalline compound obtained from a plant called nux vomica.

"It's a little more expensive than what I used to carry, but it sure works real well," the storekeeper said. "I promise you it will kill your rats and your dog, cat, and also any enemies you might want to eliminate!"

The man cackled, very much amused with his own little

joke. It was all that Kimbal could do to muster up a weak smile and murmur, "Sounds fine. What about the razor?"

"Right over here in the glass counter," the man said, his smile dying as quick as it had been born. "I got the best you'll find in Elko and the prices are fair. Need a fine leather strop, too?"

"Actually, I do," Kimbal said, relieved that he and the all-too-cheerful storekeeper had finally shifted to a new topic of conversation.

Dalton Kimbal did not remember the rest of the conversation and was only dimly aware that he bought a new razor of the finest Swiss steel and also a very expensive leather strop. Oh well, he thought, his hand clutching the sack containing his purchases, if I fail with the poison, I can use the expensive new razor to cut my own throat.

"Good night now!" the gregarious proprietor called as he pulled his Closed sign into view. "And good luck with those rats! Let me know how it works!"

"Sure thing," Kimbal mumbled as he peered into his bag and stared at the rat poison, wondering exactly how he was going to administer the lethal dose and how much it would take to kill Curly Cutter and Dan Barling. At least fifty times a rat's dosage, he supposed. Especially for Barling, who no doubt had the constitution of a draft horse.

The Ogden banker was so absorbed in this morbid rumination that he almost walked into the pair of lathered horses that came racing around the street corner and swept past. In fact, if it had not been for a shabbily outfitted cowboy who grabbed him by the shoulder and pulled him back onto the boardwalk, he would have been run down by a powerful Appaloosa stallion.

"Jesus, mister!" the cowboy swore as the horses raced by in the darkness. "You got to watch where you're walking around here! That big stud horse would have ground you up in the dirt!"

Dalton Kimbal was staring at the galloping horses. He saw them being reined in down at the end of the street before a livery stable and then he saw the unmistakably broad silhouette of Long Rider's shoulders. And the slender, unmistakably feminine shape of Polly Benton.

The banker began to tremble.

"Take it easy, mister. It's all right now. But I reckon you owe me your life and I would not be upset by a small financial reward."

"Huh?"

The cowboy shook his arm and peered right up close into the banker's face. "I said that I had saved your life and that it ought to be worth something. I mean, you look like you got some money to spare for this good samaritan."

Kimbal forced himself to focus on the cowboy. "Oh . . . oh, yes!" he said. "Of course I am grateful and want to repay you."

The cowboy, who was starting to turn belligerent, suddenly cracked a half-toothless smile. "I'll hold that package for you."

"No!" Kimbal swallowed. He had spoken too sharply again. "I mean, I can handle it."

He managed to get his wallet out and extract a bill, not even checking to see its denomination.

The cowboy whistled with appreciation through the gap in his teeth. "Well, thank you, mister! I didn't expect no fifty dollars, but I sure can use it!"

Before Kimbal could react in protest, the cowboy was moving away and the banker quickly turned his attention back to Long Rider and Polly. He saw them lead their sweating horses into the barn and vanish from his sight.

Kimbal hurried straight across the street and entered the saloon where he'd find Cutter and Barling. He completely forgot that he was carrying the rat poison he planned to eventually use on the gunslingers.

"Hey!" Curly Cutter shouted. "What are you doing in here!"

Both he and Barling had a bottle of beer in their left hands and a woman pressed up close.

"I've got to talk to you both right now!" Kimbal said breathlessly.

Barling and Cutter scowled.

"Well, as you can plainly see," Cutter said, hugging a buxom prostitute, both Dan and I are mighty busy at the moment."

"Get unbusy," Kimbal said. "There's work that has to be done right now. And there's a bonus to be earned."

Barling was interested enough to push his whore aside and ask, "How much, payable when?"

"A hundred dollars payable tonight."

"Piss on it," Cutter snarled. "I mean to enjoy myself tonight."

"Then two hundred."

"Each?" Barling asked.

Kimbal nodded his head up and down rapidly.

Even Cutter seemed interested now. "You look like you seen a ghost. What the hell is wrong?"

In answer, Kimbal walked down the bar to a table that was unoccupied and would offer them some privacy. Both Cutter and Barling came down and drew up chairs.

"Spit it out, Mr. Kimbal," Barling drawled, rolling a cigarette.

"I told you never to address me by name!"

"Cut the bullshit," Cutter snapped. "You said there was a way to make two hundred each tonight. It don't take a lot of brains to guess that you just saw someone from Ogden. Who is it you need killed?"

"Gabe Conrad."

Cutter and Barling both blinked and the latter found his tongue first. "Ain't he the one they call Long Rider?"

"Yeah, that's the man. He's with Mrs. Benton. Will he recognize either one of you?"

"No," they both said decisively.

"Good," Kimbal breathed. "I don't want any connection with this job and Ogden. Understood?"

"Sure," Barling growled. "Do you want us to kill 'em both?"

Kimbal wrung his hands. "Bartender!" he shouted. "Whiskey all around!"

"I asked you a question, Mr. Kimbal. You want this Long Rider *and* the woman killed?"

Kimbal waited until the whiskey came and he could pour himself a drink. The liquor steadied him and he took several deep breaths. "I want . . . I want the man killed, yes. But not the woman. She'll be carrying a check from my bank for twelve thousand dollars. I need it back."

Cutter whistled. "Twelve thousand dollars! Jesus! And you're offering us a lousy two hundred each! Mister, you ain't dealin' with a couple of turnip heads. If the stakes are that high, we figure the job is worth at least another thousand."

Even Barling was surprised by the size of the demanded figure. But he recovered quickly and nodded his big, knife-scarred head. "That's right. Besides, I hear that this Long Rider is a tough hombre. He won't be easy to kill."

Kimbal poured himself another drink. "All right," he said hoarsely, "I'll pay the thousand dollars!"

"Each," Cutter snapped. "And before we leave Elko."

Kimbal wanted to open his bag of new store purchases and somehow shove the damned rat poison down their greedy throats. But, of course, that was impossible, and besides, when they were dying, he could get his money back as he watched their agonies.

"Agreed," he said in a weak voice. "Just do the job."

"What are we supposed to do with the woman?"

"I don't know!"

"Well," Barling said stubbornly, "if you don't want her killed, we have to do something with her."

The man was right. Kimbal removed his derby and ran his fingers through his thinning hair. "Just . . . just knock her over the head, get the check and all her money so it will look like a robbery, then let her be."

"Is she good-lookin'?" Cutter said. "If she is, I reckon big Dan and I can find a good use for her."

"No!"

Half the men in the saloon turned around when Kimbal shouted.

"All right. All right," Cutter said soothingly in a voice that was low and secretive. "I was only kidding anyway. So where are they?"

"At the livery stable at the end of the street."

Cutter pushed away from the table. "So the job is as good as done."

"Wait a minute," Kimbal whispered, trying to gather his scattered thoughts. "The important thing is that this looks like a normal robbery that resulted in a killing. I don't want any connection to me—or to Ogden. Is that one-hundred-percent clear?"

"Clear as rainwater," Barling said. He patted the banker on the shoulder with his big paw. "You just take that bottle and get on back to your hotel room. We'll come tell you as soon as the job is done."

Kimbal nodded. He did not look up, nor did he say thank you. Instead, he clutched his razor, strop, and rat poison and waited until the pair were on their way out the door. Then he poured another drink and, avoiding the curious glances he was receiving, he tossed the whiskey down and sleeved a flood of nervous sweat from his eyes.

It was going to be all right. Everything was going to work out just fine.

CHAPTER ELEVEN

Gabe studied the heavily reinforced corral where Diablo was going to spend the next four or five hours while he and Polly got some desperately needed sleep. "I don't know," he said. "It's not as good a corral as I'd like, but I think the Appaloosa is so tired and hungry that he'll eat, then rest easy until we are ready to leave."

Polly nodded wearily. "Your sorrel gelding is holding up pretty well, but that stallion is amazing. He's carrying double the sorrel's weight and pushing himself every mile."

"He's tough, all right," Gabe conceded, not trying to hide his own growing admiration for the animal. "But it's still a long way across Nevada."

As if he heard and understood, Diablo raised his head from the grain and hay that had been thrown to him and bugled a ringing challenge.

Gabe smiled. The mustang had done everything asked of him and more. But just like a clever thief, the stallion seemed to be waiting for his one best chance at revenge.

Gabe did not trust the animal any farther than he might have thrown him. "I'm going to be sleeping right here at the livery. That fresh pile of straw near the back door looks better than a feather bed."

"Then I'm sleeping here, too," Polly announced.

"But you can't do that."

"And why the devil not?" Polly asked, walking over to the pile of straw and collapsing with a sigh.

"Well . . . hell, Polly. You're a respectable woman! You can't just sleep in the hay with a fella."

She managed a weak smile. "Mister, I ache so bad and feel so tired that I wouldn't know if you made love to me tonight or not. And besides, you don't look that fresh yourself. I think my virtue is in no danger."

Gabe colored a little. "I guess I tend to worry about honest women too much. I was just thinking of appearances for your sake."

"Why don't we catch a few hours of sleep starting right now?" she asked. "We can debate the propriety of this arrangement tomorrow as we gallop another hundred miles across the desert, maybe dodging Paiute arrows or bullets."

"Suits me," Gabe said, pitching his saddle down and walking over to lie beside the woman, smelling her and the fresh straw mingle invitingly. "You're holding up mighty well, Polly. Chris would be proud of you. Not many men could have ridden as far and as fast as we have without complaint. You know that?"

But Polly was already asleep. Gabe sat up and stared at her resting in a shaft of moonlight that slanted through the back door of the livery. Almost from the moment she had fallen asleep, the deep lines of strain and fatigue he'd seen had vanished. Now, she looked like an innocent woman-child sleeping so peacefully.

Gabe reached out for his saddle blanket and covered her

because the night air was cold. Satisfied that she would not be chilled, he fell back on the straw and closed his eyes, trying to get as much precious sleep as he could during the next few hours. He'd need it tomorrow, that was for sure. The liveryman had warned him and Polly not to ride west because of the Paiute. The rampaging Indians had burned out three telegraph offices and torn down the lines for more than a hundred miles.

There were also rumors that the Paiutes had burned and pillaged at least a half dozen ranches and slaughtered every longhorn cow within the radius of a hundred miles. It seemed that there had been a treaty giving the Paiutes certain rights and protection from white intruders who kept forcing their way onto the Indian lands. The treaty had just been broken by a new army commander at Fort Deeth, and all hell had broken loose in this hard desert country.

Long Rider figured the Paiutes were probably in the right against the army and the tide of whites that were flooding across their lands. He was Oglala, but what had happened to his own people was being repeated everywhere in the West as treaties were broken and Indian lands were confiscated for the white man's ranches or profit. Indians were being forced to live on reservations that were so inhospitable that even the long-eared jackrabbit could not find enough to eat. It was a tragedy, and Gabe figured that one day it might even be considered a lasting national disgrace.

He was just starting to drift off to sleep when he thought he heard a sound that did not belong in the night. An unnatural sound. Not one that was made by the horses or mules being kept here, or by a barn cat or even a chicken. No, it had been a man-made sound.

Gabe slowed his breathing. He listened hard, hearing the soft slumber of the woman beside him and all the other sounds of the night as his mind sorted through them in search of the one that did not belong.

He heard it again and this time his left hand moved slowly across his hard, flat belly toward the gun on his hip. Because his right index finger had once been broken and was now cocked at an unnatural angle, he had become adept at handling a gun with either hand. He was about to slide his gun out of his holster when a huge man appeared in the back doorway with his gun cocked and aimed at Gabe.

"Don't even think about it," the man growled.

Gabe's hand was gripping the butt of his six-gun when a second man appeared from the front door of the barn. "Freeze, or the woman is going to die right along with you."

Gabe knew he was caught dead to rights and that he could not risk going for his gun with Polly sleeping so close beside him. "What do you want? Money? We haven't got much."

The big man said, "We got some business with you, that's all. Get up slow and easy with your hands away from your gun."

Gabe could not see their faces, only their silhouettes. He glanced sideways at Polly. "If you touch her, I'll find a way to kill you both."

"Tough talk for a man who is looking down the barrels of two six-guns," the tall one said. "Now get up or we'll riddle you both."

Gabe climbed slowly to his feet. Polly was so exhausted she was sleeping blissfully through this entire affair and Gabe hoped she would miss everything. They could do without their money until they reached Reno and cashed in the twelve-thousand-dollar check she had sewn into her boot tops.

"Who are you?" he asked. "What do you want with us?"

"I'll ask the damn questions. You just face the wall," the big man rumbled. "Turn around slow and keep those hands up. All we want is money."

"I told you, we don't have but a couple of dollars between us. If you let me get to those saddlebags, I'll get it for you."

"We'll find it ourselves," the man said. "Now shut up because if the woman wakes and starts screaming, it could get fatal."

Gabe's sleep-starved mind was struggling as if it were mired in quicksand. He could not think of a way to get the upper hand without endangering Polly's life, and nothing was worth doing that. Certainly not for the less than a hundred dollars in cash that they carried.

"Don't wake her," the tall one with the deeper voice said, his face touched for an instant by moonlight to reveal the disfiguring knife scars. "Just search those saddlebags."

"For what!" Gabe demanded. "I told you where the money—"

"Shut up," the tall man hissed.

Gabe heard the sound of their saddlebags being riffled and then the smaller man said, "It's got to be on her."

"Then search her but try not to wake her."

But Polly *did* awaken. Even with his back turned, Gabe heard her mumble as the man's hands explored her body with more than a casual interest. Polly cried out with surprise, and just as Gabe whirled, he heard the sound of a fist striking flesh. Polly grunted and then there was a muffled explosion of gunfire, and Gabe felt as if he had been kicked in the side by an army mule.

He tried to grab the tall man but there was no strength in his arms and he fell just as another gunshot boomed in his face. The acrid scent of gunpowder and smoke filled his nostrils and he dropped to the barn floor fighting to hold back a sea of spiraling darkness.

"I still can't find it!" Curly Cutter swore in frustration.

"We got to get out of here!" Barling swore. "Dammit, I didn't want to use a gun. I planned to use my knife on him!"

"Well, it's done now." Curly pitched the match into the pile of straw. The match sputtered brightly and then began to burn. "Too bad about the woman. She's a looker."

"Let's go!" Barling hissed. "Those gunshots will bring half the town running."

They both took off out the back way just as the livery-man came rushing into the barn with a lantern. When he saw the two still figures lying on the straw with flames all around them, the man swore and jumped forward. He was strong and desperate and somehow he managed to grab Polly just before the flames licked into her hair. He dragged her outside and then he went back for Long Rider.

In the intensifying firelight, he saw the blood on Gabe and almost left him to run, but he forced himself to pull Gabe out of the barn and then went back inside and began to throw open the doors of the stalls containing horses.

Mad with fright, the animals came thundering out of the burning livery, and somewhere in the night a fire bell tolled as its company scrambled to the alarm.

Gabe and Polly were aware of none of this. Not until hours later when they both awoke in the doctor's office with half the town crowded outside the door watching would they know how close they'd come to dying.

"Ask the big one if he was smoking in my barn! Maybe he lit a match and . . ."

"He didn't start the fire, you damned fool!" the doctor

swore. "No more than he shot himself twice. What's the matter with you, Ormly!"

"Well, someone has to pay for my livery!" the man wailed. "It's gone up in smoke. I'm out of business."

"Get him out of here!" the doctor shouted in anger.

The liveryman was escorted outside and his shouts woke Gabe, who blinked and then started. "Is she alive? Is Polly alive?"

He tried to sit up but changed his mind when the pain in his side threatened to send him back to oblivion. "Is she all right?"

"She's got a nasty bruise on her left cheek where some dirty son of a bitch hit her with either his gun or his fist," the doctor said. "Other than that, she's fine. You're the one that ought to be dead."

Gabe relaxed. "Let me sleep," he said. "All I need is a little sleep."

The doctor shook his head as Gabe closed his eyes. He finished cleaning out the pair of bullet wounds that had passed cleanly through the meat of Gabe's left side. "The man has just been shot twice and all he cares about is the woman and sleep. I tell you, this one is tough."

Everyone nodded. They could hear the fire bell ringing, and now that it seemed obvious the pair weren't going to be of much interest for a while, they rushed outside and watched the flames bring down the roof of the livery.

It wasn't every day that Elko had so much excitement.

"Did you get it!" Dalton Kimbal demanded as the pair crashed into his hotel room and locked the door behind themselves.

"No," Curly swore. "We searched their saddlebags but it wasn't there. I was searching her when Long Rider went crazy. After that, well, there wasn't any more time."

"Incompetent fools!" Kimbal raged. "I won't pay you for a botched job. By damned I swear I won't!"

Barling reached down and pulled his Colt. "I shot Long Rider dead. I'll do the same with you if you don't pay up, Mr. Kimbal. Now what's it to be? A bullet or the money?"

Kimbal went loose in the joints. His bowels felt watery and his mouth went to dust. "All right," he breathed. "All right!"

Barling grinned. "Nice to know that you are a man who keeps his promises, Mr. Kimbal."

"Sarcasm is not your forte," Kimbal said acidly.

"My what?"

"Never mind. Did anyone else see you?"

"No," Cutter said. "And I started a fire so there will be no evidence."

Kimbal relaxed. "Is Mrs. Benton dead?"

"It couldn't be helped," Cutter said, looking ashamed. "She saw me. I couldn't have no witnesses. It wasn't something I wanted to do."

"Then you shouldn't have grabbed her by the tits," Barling growled. "That was what woke her up."

Kimbal turned away, feeling sick to his stomach. He had always admired Polly Benton, even fantasized about making love to her. She had been a strong and desirable woman. A woman who'd deserved better than to die in a barn fire after being rudely fondled by a slimy character.

"Go back to your rooms," Kimbal ordered, suddenly almost wild to pull his derringer and kill them even though it would certainly mean his own death.

"What about the money?" Barling rumbled.

"I'll get it before we leave this town on the train! Dammit, I can't go anywhere without your protection. If that wasn't clear to you before, it sure ought to be by now."

The two men had to agree with him and they left. When

the door closed behind them, Kimbal walked over to his window and pulled a chair up beside the curtain.

By sitting off to one side, he could just see the fire roaring down at the end of the street. It seemed as though the entire town of Elko was out there fighting it, as well they should because in clapboard frontier towns like this, the whole place could go up in a single, devastating inferno.

"God help me," he muttered to himself. "I'm the cause of two more deaths. I don't care about Long Rider and I'll gladly kill those two jackals with me now, but a woman like Mrs. Benton . . . what a tragic waste!"

He bowed his head in despair and wondered if he would ever get through this nightmare alive and as rich as he had always intended to be.

Rich or dead. Dalton Kimbal figured that it would turn out one way or the other about thirty seconds after he cashed in his checks and walked out of the Frontier Bank in Reno.

CHAPTER TWELVE

The sheriff of Elko scratched his protruding belly and yawned through a set of tobacco-stained teeth. "Mister, I need a little more to go on if I'm to have any damn chance of catching the men that shot you and hurt the lady."

Long Rider sat up very slowly on the doctor's examining table. The doctor had bandaged Gabe's side tightly, and he felt shaky but determined to find the men that had nearly killed Polly and himself.

"Listen," he told the sheriff, "I explained that I didn't get a clear look at either one of them. Especially the shorter one. The big man, well, he had a lot of scars on his face. Seemed to me as if his lips were twisted by a scar or something."

The sheriff blinked. "I saw a jasper around here lately that fits that description. Big, mean-looking bastard."

Gabe eased off the doctor's table and tried to button on his shirt. "Where did you see him?"

"In Abe Ronk's saloon a couple of days ago."

"Then that's where I'm going," Gabe said. "He tried

to kill me and I had the feeling that he and his friend were after something besides money.''

Polly grabbed his arm. "Please, don't do it. You're in no shape for a fight, and we're running out of time.''

"If he isn't there, I'll be right back," Gabe promised. "I'll stop and hunt the man up on our return trip."

"Now, wait just a minute," the sheriff protested. "You ain't going after anybody in my town. I'll be the one to say who gets arrested and who don't."

Gabe turned on the sheriff with contempt. The lawman was slovenly and it was very clear that he did not want to go out of his way and perhaps run into trouble.

"I'm going over to that saloon and have a look," Gabe said, pushing to his feet.

"Lady," the sheriff said, looking to Polly to help. "This man of yours is askin' for more trouble than he can handle in his condition."

Polly's left eye was half swollen shut and darkly bruised. "Then I'd better go along with him," she snapped as she took Gabe's arm and escorted him outside.

"Well, go ahead and get yourselves shot if that's what you're so damned determined to do!" the sheriff bellowed in their wake.

When they reached the saloon, Gabe plucked Polly's hand from his arm and said, "I'd feel better if you'd stay out here and wait."

Polly produced a derringer from her skirts. "Not a chance."

Gabe shrugged and loosed his own gun in its holster before he stepped through the bat-wing doors. Due to the activity created by the fire, business was off at the moment and there were only a few men standing along the bar. When they saw Gabe and Polly with her swollen eye, conversation died.

"He's not here," Gabe said to Polly before he turned

back to the bartender and the curious customers. "Listen up!"

He had their full attention so he proceeded. "This woman and I were just passing through your town tonight when we were set upon at the livery. Mrs. Benton was beaten as you can see, and I was shot. Maybe even worse from your point of view, someone burned down the livery, and it could just as easily have been the whole town."

"What do you want from us?" the bartender asked.

"One of the men that did it is tall, big shouldered, and his face is knife scarred. He was seen drinking in here. I want to know where he went."

"Beats me," the bartender said. "Customers come and go."

"Maybe, but tell that big man that I'll recognize him when I pass back this way again, and I'll gun him down on sight." Gabe's voice was steel. "You tell him to stick around Elko until I come through again. Understand?"

There wasn't a man in the room who didn't doubt that Gabe could do exactly what he'd promised. Blood had seeped through his shirt and he looked terrible in his anger and need for revenge. "If I see the man again, I'll tell him," the bartender promised. "But when you come back, please don't try and kill him in here and shoot up my place."

Gabe wheeled, took Polly's arm, and they left the saloon. Maybe issuing a warning had been the wrong thing to do if he really wanted his man but then, on the other hand, it was a challenge and to ignore it would brand his assailant a coward and perhaps keep him waiting in Elko for a showdown.

"Let's saddle up and ride," Gabe said. "We've already overstayed."

"Are you sure that you can go on?" Polly looked deeply

concerned. "Gabe, I won't have you killing yourself for me and the ranch."

"I'll make it," he said. "I've been shot a lot worse and made it."

Gabe stopped in the middle of the street. The flames had died, leaving a massive bed of coals. A few sparks were still flying, and the firemen were running around drinking beer and pissing them out. Everyone in town looked relieved as well as happy, the sole exception being the livery owner himself.

Gabe shook his head at the sight, then turned to Polly, whose poor eye was almost swollen completely shut now. "Come here," he said.

Polly came to his side. Gabe bent over and very gently kissed her swollen eye. "Don't worry another second about me. We'll both get to Reno before the Union Pacific can bring the bad tidings from Ogden."

"But we've still got so far to go and you've been shot twice."

"Hell," Gabe said with more confidence than he felt. "They don't call me Long Rider for nothing."

"Why do they call you that?" Polly asked, looking as if she wanted to return his kiss.

"It's a long story. Tell you later," he said, pivoting on his heel and heading toward the corral, where the Appaloosa was pacing around in circles.

Gabe peeked through the fence and said, "Diablo, I just hope you aren't so rested now that you want to give me problems tonight."

Diablo stomped a forefoot hard on the ground. There was fire in his eyes and for an instant Gabe strongly considered turning the animal free and trying to make it across Nevada on a lesser horse. But that would pretty much assure that their race with the Union Pacific would be lost.

And if there was anything that Gabe didn't like, it was getting beat by men, broncs, women, or iron horses.

Upstairs in a hotel room, angry words were being spoken.

"He saw me, damn you!" Barling raged. "The man went into the saloon and told everyone that he saw me and he was coming back to gun me down!"

"So what!" Curly Cutter argued. "It means nothing. You'll be in Reno in five more days and we can track him down there."

"No," Barling said, picking up his rifle. "I'm going after him."

"Are you crazy?" Cutter exclaimed. "Dan, there are Indians out there looking for both our scalps! Remember that cute little squaw we found gathering pine nuts the last time we rode out that way?"

"Of course I do. But that's history."

"History, my ass! What we done to her probably started this damn Paiute war!"

"No one ever saw us," Dan swore. "And I'll be following Long Rider. If he runs into the Paiutes, they'll kill him for me."

Curly shook his head. "Maybe, but if you get killed, I'm just going to take the whole damn thousand dollars that Kimbal has promised us."

"If I get killed," Barling growled, making sure his gear was in order, "then it ain't going to matter a damn bit to me if you get the money or if that sidewinding banker manages to kill you first. 'Cause you know that's what Kimbal plans to do."

"Yeah, I know that," Cutter said tightly. "I just don't see why you can't stay here and wait for the train takin' us on to Reno. Hell, you might not even be able to overtake Long Rider and his woman."

"Sure, I will," Barling said, heading out the door. "I got a hell of a horse and I'll back-shoot the man before noon tomorrow. Then I'll have the woman for myself, and when I'm done with her, even the Indians won't be interested."

Now Curly understood. "So, it's the woman you really want."

"You got it figured. That, and a twelve-thousand-dollar check she's carrying on her somewheres."

Curly blinked. "Son of a bitch! I forgot about that!"

"It's because your brains have always been below your belt," the big man growled.

At the door, he turned and lowered his voice. "When Kimbal discovers I went after them two, he's gonna be madder than hell. You keep a close eye on him and don't turn your back on him for a second."

"He's safe enough until I get him to that bank in Reno," Curly said. "He's afraid that someone on the next train will be from Ogden and recognize him. He'll need me to handle that little problem if it comes up."

"Yeah," Barling said. "I expect that's true enough. After I kill Long Rider and spend a day or so pleasuring myself with the woman, I'll come back in time to board the train. And this way, we won't have to worry about a welcoming committee in Reno. Savvy?"

"Savvy," Curly said, sticking out his hand, which was engulfed by Barling's immense paw. "You just ambush that bastard. He's already got two of your bullets in him and damned if I know how he survived. But now you'll be shooting a rifle, and that'll do the job."

Barling winked. "I ain't only taking this one, I know where I can find me a fifty-two-caliber Sharps buffalo rifle. It'll knock him out of the saddle at a half mile, if the wind is right."

Curly giggled. "He's as good as dead already, Dan.

He's meat for the coyotes and rattlesnakes. Sure as hell, he is! I just wish I could be there to share the woman with you.''

Barling shook his head. ''You shouldn't have grabbed her by the tits,'' he said. ''If she hadn't woke up screaming, this whole mess wouldn't have happened and Long Rider would have already been dead and tossed in some ravine. Now, I'm paying for your mistake.''

Curly lowered his eyes. ''I couldn't help myself,'' he muttered. ''She's just such a damn good looker.''

''I know,'' the big man said. ''That's why *I'm* going after them instead of you.''

Dan Barling wasted no time in picking up a buffalo rifle from a man he knew in town. The rifle was in good condition and Barling was well familiar with the model, for he had hunted buffalo for the Union Pacific when it had been built a number of years earlier.

''I'll take good care of it,'' he told the man as he tightened the cinch on his saddle.

''You find some buffalo?''

''Hell, no.''

''Gizzly bear?''

''Nope.''

The man shook his head. ''Then you're gonna kill some Paiutes, I suspect.''

''You're getting warmer,'' Barling said.

''Listen,'' the man said. ''If you want to get yourself scalped, that's your affair. But that's my rifle you're toting and it's worth every bit of a hundred dollars of any man's money. You can see that it's like brand new.''

''Yep.''

''So I want the money.''

Barling shoved the big-bored rifle into its scabbard and

tied it securely under his left stirrup fender. "I thought you was loanin' it to me, Zeke."

Zeke was a plump man without any chin. He had a three-day growth of beard and a two-day hangover. "I changed my mind. I thought you was just going to hunt a little game. I can see that you're after men." He straightened. "I need the money. You can have the hundred back if I get the rifle returned in good condition."

"You'll drink the money up before I get back," Barling said quietly.

"Maybe so and maybe not. But I still want it."

"All right," Barling said. "You want to get paid off, here you go."

He acted as if he were reaching inside his coat pocket to get his wallet, but instead he pulled his knife from its sheath. It had a four-inch blade, thin and sharpened on both sides, and when it came out of its sheath, it seemed to come alive in Barling's big hand.

"Here you go, Zeke," he said quietly as his hand extended. "Payment in full."

Zeke reached for what he thought was money. Too late, the smaller man realized that the wicked dagger blade was moving directly for his soft belly. He cried out in alarm as Barling drove four inches of steel into his abdomen, then ripped the blade upward, gutting him like a deer.

"Son of a bitch!" Zeke wailed, his hands fluttering upward to clasp Barling's powerful wrist. "Oh, you son of a bitch!"

Barling was so powerful that he lifted the skewered man right off his feet and seemed to hold him suspended several inches off the ground before he yanked the knife free and let Zeke fall.

"There you are," he said. "Paid in full, just like you asked for."

Zeke groaned and his bootheels raked the earth a few times before his body lay still.

Barling wiped his knife on the dead man's shirt, then regarded him coldly. "You shoulda give me the rifle and kept your mouth shut," he said before he jammed his boot into the stirrup and swung into the saddle.

The tall bay mare he rode was a Thoroughbred-Morgan cross, so it had speed and endurance. Barling treasured his horse and had won many a race on the mare.

He would pick up Long Rider's trail just west of town, and he was pretty sure the man would follow the rails all the way to Reno. It wasn't the most direct route, but it was the best. There were water towers and maybe a few railroad shacks if they had not been all burned to the ground by the marauding Indians.

One thing Barling was dead sure of was that there wasn't no woman alive that could keep up a pace that would leave him and his bay mare far behind. He'd catch them, all right. If the Paiutes didn't catch them first.

CHAPTER THIRTEEN

Gabe watched the sunrise break and spill over the Ruby Mountains and he felt the Appaloosa shift between his long legs, then continue drinking in the lazy Humboldt River.

Beside him, Polly had dismounted and was crouched down, splashing water in her face. "I can't keep my eyes open much longer," she said. "Correction. My *eye* open," she amended.

Gabe said, "The swelling is going down. Besides, one eye sees as far as two."

"That's not very comforting."

Polly stood and gripped her saddle horn as the water swirled up to her knees. "As cold as this is, I'm so numb with weariness it might as well be bath water. We have to stop pretty soon, Gabe. Diablo looks good for another hundred miles without a rest, but your sorrel is favoring his right front foot and he's all played out."

"I know that," Gabe said. "He's got a rock bruise and there's nothing that can be done for it. That packing I put up tight against his frog helps, but the only thing that will cure him is rest and time. I'm afraid that we're a little short on both of them.''

"How far is it to Fort Deeth?"

"About forty miles, I'd say."

Gabe's gray eyes slowly studied the landscape and his brow was knit with worry. "I've had this feeling for the last quarter hour or so that we're being watched."

Polly's head snapped up and she looked all around. "Indians?"

"Afraid so," Gabe said. "But since I haven't spotted them yet, I can't say for sure."

Polly climbed quickly back into her saddle. "We'd better get out of here!"

Gabe agreed. "We'll just stay down along this river. If the Paiutes show, we'll try to make a run for it."

"I should never have let you talk us into this," Polly said nervously. "No, that's not true. *I* would have talked us into it if you hadn't. But if we get scalped I'll never forgive you."

"I'll try to remember that," Gabe said, pulling the stallion's head up and touching its flank with his spurs.

The big Appaloosa reined pretty good, though always with the hint of resistance. Still, Gabe could not complain about the animal's behavior. It made no pretense of liking him, but there was a mutual respect between them, and even after three days of riding, the mustang acted fresh. It reminded Gabe all over again that nothing grew stronger than animals left wild and unprotected by man.

They stayed close beside the water and several times Gabe saw the hoofprints of unshod Indian ponies in the sand. He knew very little about the Paiute. He had been raised by Plains Indians who were buffalo hunters. The Paiutes were desert Indians, and they had long ago been forced to adapt to an entirely different life-style in order to eke out a meager existence.

The Paiute, Gabe supposed, would hunt rabbit and the few deer they could find in the nearby mountains. Maybe they also planted and harvested a little corn and irrigated it with water from their few and precious rivers such as this Humboldt, which the first whites had followed in their covered wagons on the way to Oregon and California.

Whatever these Indians did to survive, Gabe knew that he would not understand either their language or their customs. He did think that he would be able to converse with them in sign language enough to explain his reason for crossing their land and to make it very clear that he was sympathetic to their plight. After all, his own Sioux people under Red Cloud had also been swindled out of their lands, then hunted down and confined to a reservation.

As if she could read Long Rider's thoughts, Polly drew her horse near and said, "Are you thinking of a speech that will keep us from being scalped?"

"I haven't gotten that far with it yet," Gabe admitted. "And to tell you the truth, I don't know if they'd believe me. After all, my eyes and hair are almost as light as yours. Besides that, this country is as foreign to a Plains Indian as anything I could imagine."

"Why would they even choose to stay here?"

"They probably had no choice," Gabe said. "In terms of seizing and holding on to a territory, Indians were pretty much like whites from what I can determine. Stronger tribes dominated weaker tribes and took the best hunting lands. My guess is that the Paiute were driven off the good lands by maybe the Ute or maybe the Shoshoni, who were in turn driven off the Plains by my people and the Cheyenne."

Polly nodded with understanding. "Well, it's hard to

imagine anyone who wants to drive them off this kind of land.''

"The whites do," Gabe said. "They always want more land. Even desert land like this."

"Why?"

"I don't know," he said. "I guess that you could run a lot of cattle along this river. And I've heard it said that these hard Nevada hills are full of gold and silver. You've heard of what happened on the Comstock Lode. It's turning out to be an even bigger strike than the one in California. And with the railroad coming through Nevada, there's just bound to be people thinking about ways to make this country pay off.''

Polly said nothing. She guessed that Gabe was right. He had told her before that the Indians, while they claimed land or hunting ground by the force of their will or by the white man's treaty, never really believed that they owned it. To the Indian's way of thinking, land was only meant to be used with respect, not to be possessed or exploited for its gold, timber, or water.

They rode on for another hour before Gabe pulled the stallion up short. "Here they come," he said grimly.

"Then we should run!"

"Where to?" he asked. "They've got rifles and they've cut us off from either the fort or from going back to Elko. If we broke and ran, they'd shoot our horses out from under us before we had covered a mile.''

"You mean they'd shoot this sorrel out from under me," Polly said. "You'd get away on Diablo and we both know it.''

It was true. Alone, Gabe would not have hesitated to make a break for open country. On Diablo, he was sure he could have succeeded in getting away cleanly. "Polly, if I thought for one minute that Diablo would let you ride him . . .''

"No," she said quietly. "I got you into this. It's my ranch that we are trying to save. I'm not leaving you here on a rock-bruised horse to face these people alone."

Long Rider felt a surge of pride for the woman. "Just don't make any sudden moves, and if they take your reins, don't try and fight them. Understand?"

Polly swallowed as she nodded her head. Now that she could plainly see the Paiutes riding forward with their hard, unforgiving faces streaked with warpaint, she struggled to hide the fear that clutched at her heart.

When the Indians came to within fifty yards, Gabe raised his hand in greeting and made sign to indicate that he was the adopted son of an Oglala Sioux warrior and had been accepted by that tribe. He told them that his name was Long Rider and then he removed his buffalo coat and showed them the sign that had been made by his mother.

The Paiute drew their horses up to a line as they studied the yellow sign of the Oglala. Several whispered and nodded and Gabe hoped that meant that they recognized the symbol. There were about thirty of them altogether, though Gabe did not turn and count the ones behind him. He instead concentrated on the ones before him and particularly on the leader.

The leader was dressed no differently than the warriors he led. In fact, a white man who did not understand the way of Indians would not have guessed which warrior was this party's chosen war chief. But Gabe had no trouble making the distinction. The man had the proud bearing of a natural leader. He was big for a Paiute, probably five foot ten at least and barrel chested. He wore five eagle feathers in his hair, more than any of the other warriors and each represented an enemy he had either slain or counted coup upon.

His nose had long ago been broken and his black hair was chopped off at his wide shoulders. He gripped a very good Henry repeating rifle in his left hand and his reins in his right. His horse was a stallion, black in color, and it pawed nervously and then squealed in challenge at the far more powerful Diablo.

Gabe held the Appaloosa in check. Again, he made sign explaining that he was Oglala and wished no trouble with his red brothers.

The leader studied him with hard, deep-set eyes for several minutes before he studied Polly. In jerky, rapid sign language, he asked who the white woman was.

She is my woman! Gabe replied in sign.

You are both whites and we are at war with the whites, the leader signed. My name is Standing Bear. You and the woman must die.

Gabe did not even blink when this pronouncement, punctuated with guttural sounds, came to him.

"It's not going very well, is it," Polly whispered so only he could hear.

Gabe ignored her. He watched Standing Bear, waiting for a signal to his warriors that would begin a bloodbath. Gabe figured he could kill at least four of these men before they killed him—if it really had to come to that.

He made one last try to avoid bloodshed. Who is the chief of your people? I want to speak to your chief. It is my right as one warrior to another among men of honor.

Standing Bear was not pleased. He shook his head emphatically with the same meaning as would a white man.

Yes! Gabe signed, his hand moving rapidly and with the same decisiveness that Standing Bear had displayed. It is my right as a warrior to meet another warrior's chief before I am sentenced to die. It *is* a matter of honor.

Standing Bear glared malevolently at him. His hand tightened on the breech of his rifle. Gabe could read deep in his eyes that the man wanted to end the talk and begin to kill.

But he could not. Gabe had called upon his honor and there was no choice but to grant his request. Standing Bear slashed his hand down and grunted something. Two warriors detached themselves from the line and rode forward. One grabbed the sorrel's reins and tore them from Polly's hand. The other warrior, who could not have been more than fifteen, made the mistake of riding in close to Diablo and reaching out to grab the stallion's reins.

The Appaloosa's jaws opened and its big yellow teeth clamped on the young warrior's leg with all the gentleness of a bear trap. The warrior yelped in pain and tried to pull his leg free. Diablo released the leg and bit the warrior's pony on the neck. The pony spun away in fear, leaving the injured warrior straddling nothing but empty air.

The warrior landed hard, grabbed his leg, and writhed with pain. He was wearing heavy woolen pants but Gabe could see blood seeping through them, so he dismounted and, ignoring Standing Bear and the others, drew his knife and slit the warrior's pants to reveal a terribly bruised and bloodied calf.

He looked down into the warrior's suffering eyes and began to make sign not only to the injured warrior, but also for the benefit of all the other Paiutes.

My horse, he said, is very strong and fast but also very mean. He must be forgiven for he is brave and angry not to be free to run with his mares, like you and your people have always been free to roam this country.

The young warrior nodded and allowed Gabe to use his handkerchief to tie a bandage around the leg and then help him back on his horse.

To Gabe's surprise, the young warrior said, "I am Temesca, son of Spotted Horse, leader of the Paiute people. You speak English?"

"I sure do!"

"Good, so does my father, but not as good as me. You

will follow us and keep the stallion away from Standing Bear, who would shoot him if it bit his leg.''

Gabe nodded. He had figured as much from the look on Standing Bear's face, though he suspected the leader of this war party could not help but respect the spirit of the great Appaloosa stallion.

Polly visibly relaxed. ''You and I must be leading charmed lives for the moment,'' she said.

''I'd hold that judgment until we speak with their chief,'' Gabe said as he mounted. ''But I'll tell you this one thing, I think Diablo's black heart and vicious ways may have just saved our bacon.''

A moment later, they were being led west, away from the river into the low, sun-blasted hills covered with juniper and pinion pine, sage and rock. They left both the river and the rails far behind and climbed higher into the desert. Gabe could not help but wonder if he or Polly would ever live to see the Humboldt River and the Union Pacific rails again.

And no one, not even the wary Paiutes, saw the big man on the bay mare that watched them closely and then remounted to follow once he was certain that he himself had not been seen.

CHAPTER FOURTEEN

Gabe supposed he should have been worrying about what he was going to say to Chief Spotted Horse, but he wasn't. For one thing, Temesca was on his side and the chief's friendly son was bound to exert a strong influence. And for another thing, Gabe knew that the Paiute weren't a tribe who enjoyed fighting, such as their brothers, the fierce Apache. Everything he had heard about the Paiute suggested instead a people that were desperately trying to cling to a hard way of life.

What did greatly concern Gabe was the time that he was losing. If the Paiute stronghold they were going to was many miles from the railroad, then it would mean he and Polly would lose precious hours in their race against the Union Pacific Railroad across Nevada.

How much time did they have left? Gabe figured that the train from Ogden would pull into Reno in less than five days. If he lost a full day with these Paiute trying to talk his way free, then he and Polly were going to be in serious trouble.

"How much farther?" he asked young Temesca.

The chief's son twisted around on his pony. He looked at Gabe and then pointed to a place in the sky where the sun would have dropped when they arrived. Gabe measured the sky and estimated he had less than an hour to go.

"I sure hope we can get out of this tonight," he told Polly. "If we cut across country we can intercept the rails and not lose more than half a day."

Polly reflected her amazement. "Here I am worried about losing our scalps and the only thing you're worried about is losing a few hours of traveling time. Is there something that you know and are not telling me?"

"I think that these are good people who don't want to hurt us," Gabe said.

"I hope you're right," Polly whispered. "But if the chief is anything like Standing Bear, my guess is that we are done for."

Gabe said nothing as the Paiutes led them into a deep arroyo that brought them halfway up a mountainside before it leveled off into a grove of pinion pine and rocks.

The Paiute village was smaller than Gabe had expected. He saw about forty rough huts made of sticks and brush. There were only a few old horses, which told Gabe that all the warriors were out and that this was a poor village but one that could be moved very quickly if danger approached.

As their group entered the village, several large dogs came bounding forward and when they saw Gabe and Polly, they began to growl and nip at their horses' hocks.

Diablo lashed out at a particularly large and vicious dog with his right hind hoof and connected solidly. Not content with that, the stallion's ears flattened and it lunged forward to finish the dog before it could recover.

The dog was knocked rolling into an old squaw who

had been chattering at Polly in a voice that sounded like breaking twigs. When the squaw saw the huge stallion charge, she shrieked and showed amazing quickness as she scuttled out of the way. It was all that Gabe could do to pull Diablo up short.

The dog must have belonged to Standing Bear because the warrior reined his horse around and threw his rifle to his shoulder. Gabe, still trying to get the stallion under control, caught a glimpse of the warrior but was too occupied to draw his gun in time.

"No!" a loud voice cut through the air and made Standing Bear freeze.

There was no mistaking Chief Spotted Horse, who began to castigate Standing Bear for almost firing a shot that could have revealed their place of hiding if any army scouts were nearby.

For a moment, the two Indians locked wills, and it was the old chief who prevailed because Standing Bear said something angry but slashed his rifle across the rump of his own horse and raced on through the village.

Gabe pulled Diablo's head up close and wound the animal's reins around his saddle horn so that the stallion did not bite him in the back while he spoke to the chief.

As he had an hour before to Standing Bear and his war party, Gabe now introduced himself as Long Rider, and while the tribe listened, he again explained his situation and the reason why they were racing across Nevada. He ended by saying very clearly in English, "I am a friend of the Indian. My own people, the Oglala, have also fought the whites."

Chief Spotted Horse had listened carefully. Now he said, "And have you also fought the whites?"

"I have," Long Rider said. "When they came against my people, I fought them at the great Wagon Box Fight

and also at Fort Fetterman, where we killed many blue-
coats.''

"I have heard of those great battles, I think," the Paiute
chief said. "But your people also fought Yellow Hair and
his soldiers at Little Big horn. Were you there under the
great war chiefs Sitting Bull and Red Cloud?"

"No," Gabe said. "But the great Red Cloud is my un-
cle, and I have always tried to make him proud. Crazy
Horse is my blood brother."

Spotted Horse was impressed. The old chief translated
the dialogue for Standing Bear, who had dismounted and
joined them. Now he challenged Gabe with his dark, suspicious eyes and with slashes of his hand said, How do
we know that this is true?

I have already shown you the sign of my buffalo coat,
Gabe answered the glowering warrior in sign language.
Now, I will show you the buffalo vest that I made from
my mother's tepee and which has great power for me.

He went to his saddlebags and took out the leather vest
that he had salvaged after the death of his mother from the
charred remnants of her tepee. He displayed the symbol
of his mother's lodge to all the Paiutes.

Having satisfied the suspicions of Standing Bear, Gabe
addressed Chief Spotted Horse and his son in English.
"And this you must also know," Gabe said, bringing out
his smoking pipe.

Gabe's pipe was longer than those the white men smoked
and its bowl was made from red stone found only at a
sacred quarry in a place the whites called Minnesota. The
stem was made from a hollowed willow branch.

As the Paiutes watched him carefully, Gabe filled the
bowl of his pipe with dried willow bark, which his people
called, *chanshasha*. Oblivious now of the Paiute, he lit it
and then, holding the bowl in his left hand and the stem
in his right, he respectfully presented the smoking pipe to

the spirits in the West, North, East and South. Satisfied, he then extended the pipe downward to the earth and finally lifted it to the great blue Nevada sky.

With the upraised pipe held aloft, a deep calmness entered Gabe to caress his spirit and to give him a sense of great power. All Indians understood this, though the whites smoked for reasons only they understood.

After a long moment in which Gabe offered the smoke to Wakan-Tanka, the Indian's Great Spirit, he lowered the pipe and handed it to the Paiute chief, who repeated the ritual and then smoked before passing it on to the elders of his tribe, who each in turn smoked the pipe before it was returned to Long Rider.

"Glad you didn't ask me to smoke it," Polly whispered.

Gabe ignored the comment. He supposed that Polly Benton was confused, bewildered, and even skeptical of the power of smoke and the strength it gave to Indians. That did not matter. All that mattered was that the Paiutes now knew with dead certainty that, despite Long Rider's gray eyes and sandy hair, in his heart, he was a warrior.

"You speak the truth, Long Rider," the chief said. "And I think that the Great Spirit sends you to help my people."

Gabe had not expected this. "I am a stranger here."

"You are one of the Native People as well as being a white man," Spotted Horse said slowly. "You must speak to the soldiers. Tell them that my people do not want war. Tell them that we will be at peace if they protect our lands and our pine nuts."

"Your what?"

Temesca interrupted to explain more fully. "Long Rider, you are Oglala and so you do not understand. The pinion pines you see here are our main food. But with all the whites coming into our lands, they are cutting down the pinion and we are starving. They use the trees for their fires and set them deep inside their caves.''

Gabe understood that *caves* was Temesca's word for *mines* and that the trees were being used for underground timbering. "Is that all I should tell the soldiers?"

"Tell them that two white men found one of our women harvesting pine nuts alone," the chief's son said with a bitterness. "They violated her and then they killed her. We demand justice for this!"

Gabe glanced at Polly and then to the chief. "Did anyone see these men?"

The chief shook his head. His eyes burned. "We found many signs and this," he said, taking a leather button out of his pocket. "These men killed our woman with a knife."

Something clicked in Gabe's mind. He could not help but think of the pair who had almost killed him and Polly in the livery barn while they rested in Elko. The tall one had the knife scars of a man who preferred the blade to the bullet.

"Chief Spotted Horse, it is not the usual way that white men kill," Gabe said. "But then, I am sure that they did not want to make a sound that could be heard by the People."

Temesca stepped forward. "My father does not say who this woman was. It was my sister, Sonseca. She was also Standing Bear's wife and she was good."

Gabe refrained from looking at Standing Bear but now he understood the hatred and outright suspicion shown by the warrior leader.

"I'm sure that she was," Polly said. "Did you tell this to the soldiers?"

"To one soldier man, yes," Temesca said in a hard voice. "But when he said my sister was not worthy of revenge, we fought and I beat him."

Gabe expelled a deep breath and looked to the chief. "What would you have us do?"

"Go to Fort Deeth," Spotted Horse said. "Tell them what you have learned and that we want peace. But they *must* find the men who killed Sonseca! And they must give these men to us."

"They would never agree to that," Gabe said. "But if I can get them to promise that these men will be punished, would this satisfy your pain and bring peace to your heart?"

The chief stood as still as granite stone for a long, long time, then, his eyes turned to his son and finally to Standing Bear. Gabe could read the chief's thoughts. Sonseca had been his daughter but she had been Standing Bear's woman. This latter relationship was the more important, and the chief, in his own language, asked the warrior if imprisonment would be enough for his wife's killers.

Standing Bear's face twisted hideously and his lips drew back from his teeth. He knew enough English to scream. "Death!"

Gabe felt Polly touch his arm and he knew she was suddenly afraid. Gabe nodded to Standing Bear. He did not blame the warrior because, had men raped and killed his wife, nothing short of their death would have been sufficient.

"I will demand that the soldiers keep the whites from cutting down your pinion pine trees. I will also ask them to look for Sonseca's killers. I can do no more," he said to the chief and his son.

"Then go," the chief said.

Gabe did not have to be told twice. He packed his pipe and his leather vest back into his saddlebags, then he quickly mounted beside Polly.

"When this is over," he said, motioning toward Polly,

"I will come back to help if it is important to peace. You cannot fight the white soldiers and win."

The chief looked up at Long rider and said, "Did Crazy Horse tell you this before or after he had Yellow Hair's scalp hanging from his war lance?"

"General Custer was not scalped," Gabe said. "He fought well as did most of his soldiers."

"Long Rider, take your woman and go now to Fort Deeth and tell them our words," Spotted Horse said. "Tell them we will keep fighting until the death if the soldiers come for us. It is better to die than to become like the white man's sheep. Is this not so?"

"I cannot say," Long Rider told the man in all honesty. "I swore to my mother that I would learn the white man's ways. Jim Bridger took me to their cities and I learned that some there are many good whites. Because there are so many, there are also many bad ones. Let us hope that the bad ones all die."

"Did you dance the Ghost Dance to rid the earth of all white men?" Temesca asked suddenly.

Gabe reined the Appaloosa stallion west and just before he touched spurs, he said, "No, because I did not believe in its power."

Polly followed him out of the Paiute camp and they rode across country heading southwest to intersect the Union Pacific rails. And as they went, they again came back into Dan Barling's rifle sights.

CHAPTER FIFTEEN

Dan Barling rode hard and steadily through the falling darkness. His tall, swift mare seemed to float across the desert floor and, as always, she was eager to run. To Barling's right, the gleaming railroad tracks stood out very sharply in the moonlight. Far to his left, he could see the luminescent glow of fresh snow on Sonoma Peak, and he judged its level would fall considerably if a winter storm overtook them.

He heard a coyote's lonesome howl somewhere out in the night and he hoped that the good weather would hold until he could overtake Long Rider and the woman, then kill them and return to Elko.

At midnight, the big assassin saw the distant, bobbing light of an onrushing locomotive and he rode toward it for nearly an hour along the flat land before the eastbound train suddenly rushed at him and then roared past.

Barling's fast bay mare skittered and her eyes rolled wildly at the sight and smell of the coal-burning locomotive. Sparks blazed from the train's stack and drifted down on the desert, the man, and his running mare. For a long time after the train passed, smoke lingered in the cold desert air, and then the approaching storm swept it away better than an invisible broom.

How far were Long Rider and the pretty woman still ahead? he kept asking himself as he followed the Humboldt River through a series of low, treeless hills. How could they still be ahead, given his own unrelenting pace? And yet, Barling knew the answer to his impatient question because he had seen Long Rider's magnificent Appaloosa and the fine sorrel gelding that the woman rode by his side.

But he would overtake them. He could tell by the sorrel's tracks that it was going lame in the right forefoot. It was only a matter of time before Long Rider had to stop and either turn the sorrel loose, or else try to ride the Appaloosa double and lead the lame gelding.

Only a matter of time.

Barling clutched the heavy stock of the buffalo rifle. He was angry at himself for not using the rifle soon after the pair had left the Paiute village. But then, if he had, he'd have been forced to outrun those Indians. And while he was sure that his bay mare possessed enough speed, a man never knew when his horse might suddenly pull up lame or step into a prairie dog hole and snap its leg. So he'd held his fire, and now he was riding a lot farther and faster than he'd expected.

Patience, he told himself. Killing the man and using the woman would make it all worthwhile. Especially using the woman. Barling had not enjoyed a woman since the young Paiute squaw he and Curly Cutter had raped and murdered.

Through the long night the wind stiffened, and by dawn the sun floated sluggishly into a gray, freezing sky and it could not muster any warmth at all. But Barling scarcely noticed. The tracks were getting fresher every mile and he was closing on his quarry.

At midmorning, Barling spotted his prey and grinned wolfishly as the wind tore at this face with pellets of ice. Let it storm. That way, he could come almost upon them before the man called Long Rider would know he was about to die. The weather was bad and the damned mare was cantankerous because she was in heat, but his luck was good.

A mile ahead, Long Rider pulled the Appaloosa stallion up and dismounted. He checked the sorrel's hoof and then its slender foreleg. "If we keep pushing this horse, we're going to do him permanent damage."

"Then let's unsaddle him and turn him loose," Polly replied.

"And how are you going to get to Reno? Run on foot?"

"No," Polly said, "we will ride the stallion double."

Gabe's mouth turned down at the corners. "He might allow it and he might not. I guess the time has come to find out. This is much too fine a gelding to cripple for life. Not worth trying to take him another ten, maybe even twenty miles."

Polly dismounted and they very quickly unsaddled the sorrel, then removed its bridle and turned the animal free. The sorrel did not run, but stood waiting as if it did not know what to do.

"Find yourself some shelter from this biting wind," Gabe told the animal. "Then find some grass along this river and eat and rest. You're free, horse."

The sorrel hurt too badly to act pleased by his sudden freedom. He shook his head and stood patiently waiting for something to happen.

Gabe remounted and then drew the stallion's head up close to its chest and dallied his latigo reins around his saddle horn. "Hand me your saddlebags," he said. "Then shove your boot into the stirrup and let's see what happens."

Polly did exactly as she was told. Because she was short and the Appaloosa stood well over sixteen hands, she had difficulty getting her foot up and in the stirrup until Gabe reached out and grabbed her by the upper arm. With a tremendous heave, he pulled her up behind him just as the Appaloosa tried to start bucking.

"Hang on!" he shouted.

Polly wrapped her arms around his waist and held on very tight. The Appaloosa didn't like the extra weight on his back and he began to buck and squeal, but Gabe used his spurs and kept his head high enough so that the bucking lacked authority.

Diablo stopped bucking and Gabe lined him out down the tracks. "Easy as could be," he called back to the woman hugging his hard belly.

Polly risked looking back over her shoulder to see the sorrel gelding as it tried to keep up with them.

"Gabe!" she cried. "There's a man galloping after us!"

He twisted around, though he had all he could handle keeping Diablo's head up and his legs moving in a straight line. Gabe caught a glimpse of a big man on a tall bay horse about a mile behind them. But most interesting of all, the big man had a big rifle clenched in his hands.

"Yaw!" Gabe shouted, loosening tension on the reins and hoping like hell that Diablo would run hard instead of starting to buck now that he had free rein.

The mustang stallion cooperated this time. Instead of bucking, it ran as if the witches of hell were on its tail.

"Are we leaving him far behind?" Gabe shouted.

"No," Polly cried. "In fact, he's gaining."

Gabe found that incredible, but when he twisted around in his saddle, he saw that it was true. Whoever the big man with the rifle was, he had himself one hell of a running horse.

The way Gabe had it figured, he was going to lose this race and his life. If the stallion had been fresh and not carrying double, he was sure that the swift bay could not have closed on him. But the stallion wasn't fresh and it was carrying too much weight to run hard over a long, long distance without faltering or blowing its lungs apart and dying on its feet.

Gabe had no intention of killing Diablo, and he was pretty darn certain that the man behind him would close to within a few hundred yards, then stop, dismount, and take dead aim with that big buffalo rifle he was toting. That's how Gabe himself would have done it if he had been a back shooter.

"Hang on tight," he gritted. "And when that man yanks his horse up and jumps off, then you yell a warning!"

Polly didn't ask any dumb questions. She just clung to Gabe and kept glancing back over her shoulder. "He's getting close!"

"Tell me when he jumps! No man can shoot that big a rifle with any accuracy off a running horse."

The stallion had its ears back and it was running low to the ground. Gabe could hear its hard breathing and he could feel the power of the horse and how it was giving every last ounce of its strength.

"Now!" Polly cried. "He's pulling up now!"

Gabe stood up in his stirrups and yanked the stallion's head back as he sawed on the reins. Diablo didn't want to stop and when forced to break his stride, he fought Gabe. He began to buck and Gabe dropped his reins allowing the stallion to drop his head between his legs and buck like crazy. Gabe snatched his Winchester from its saddle scabbard and a split second later he and Polly were airborne as the buffalo rifle boomed in the cold desert air.

Gabe swore he heard the huge-caliber slug pass just inches from his ear, and there was no mistaking the yelp of pain Polly made when she landed heavily in the brush.

"Stay down!" he shouted, twisting about as Diablo went tearing off.

"Of course I'm staying down! I'm not stupid, you know!"

Gabe levered a shell into his Winchester. He knew enough about weaponry to be pretty damn sure that he was up against a man with a breechloader. Probably a buffalo rifle, from the size of it. He also realized that the rifleman would be reloading the heavy single-shot rifle, which employed a paper-wrapped cartridge with ball attached.

Gabe knew the buffalo rifle well and had often used one up in Wyoming. In loading its cartridge, the trigger guard acted as a lever, which lowered the breechblock and exposed the chamber. Once the cartridge was inserted, a man slapped the breechblock back into the closed position, and this sheared off the end of the paper-wrapped cartridge, exposing the powder inside. All that was required after that was to pull the trigger, and when the percussion cap exploded, the flame would strike the powder and the gun fired.

It sounded complicated, but it really wasn't, and when a man got comfortable with one of those big rifles, he could work himself up to getting a shot off every twelve to fifteen seconds. It was fast—against buffalo—but not against a man with a Winchester repeater.

"Here," Gabe said, pulling his Colt and offering it to Polly. "You stick that up every half minute or so and pull the trigger in his general direction. Don't put your head or body up. Just keep his attention."

"Where are you going?"

"I'm going to circle around behind and catch him in a

cross fire,'' Gabe said as he moved off before she could argue. Polly was brave, smart, and resourceful. She was a hell of a horsewoman and tough as they came, but sometimes she liked to talk too damn much and she seemed mighty inclined to argue.

''But . . . Gabe!''

He was gone, moving swiftly through the brush on his hands and knees, keeping himself low and out of sight.

Gabe heard Polly fire his six-gun and then the buffalo rifle answered in a deep-throated reply. Gabe moved even faster. It seemed to take him forever to get around to the place that he wanted, and when he finally did, he had counted no less than six shots from his Colt and . . . six shots!

Gabe started with alarm. Polly would be out of bullets! He was wearing the cartridge belt!

Just then he heard Polly cry out in fear and he poked his head up to see the huge man racing toward where she was hidden. He was less than a hundred feet from her now and reloading his own rifle as he ran. He had tied the reins of his mare to his belt and she was charging after him.

An icy river of fear shot through Gabe's veins. He jumped to his feet and snapped off a shot. The big man twisted around and fell, then popped up again to fire the buffalo rifle just as Gabe jumped sideways. His Stetson sailed from his head and he felt the big slug burrow just over the flesh of his scalp like a red-hot poker. Gabe fell over backward and tried to lever another bullet into his rifle. He was dazed and he knew that he was all out of time.

Suddenly, he heard a shout and then Diablo's familiar trumpeting cry as the stallion's hoofbeats drummed the earth. Gabe pushed himself to his hands and knees and saw the stallion attack the running man, knock him flying, and then rear and stomp him twice before the Appaloosa whirled, kicked the bay mare, and then used his teeth on her to drive her up a deep arroyo.

Gabe understood what was happening in a flash of intuition born of a lifetime of working around horses. The mare was in heat and the stallion was without a harem and desperate for mares. Desperate and now, thanks to Gabe, unafraid of man. Gabe watched the two magnificent animals disappear up the arroyo and then rushed over to the knife-scarred man who lay writing in the brush.

Gabe knelt at the man's side and what he saw was not a pretty sight. Diablo's sharp front hooves had crushed the man's throat and chest so that his left side was caved in like a half-squashed box and he was strangling for lack of air. Gabe reached for the man's coat thinking he might loosen it and give him some comfort, but the big man's vision seemed to clear. With a low snarl, he grabbed a knife from up his sleeve and took a vicious swipe at Gabe, who jumped back at the very last instant and avoided getting himself ripped open.

Gabe slashed the barrel of his Winchester down on the man's wrist and the knife dropped from his fingers. "You're the same man that attacked us in Elko, aren't you." It was not a question because no one would have mistaken this man's disfigured face that Gabe had seen as the moonlight streamed into the livery.

Polly came up and when she saw that face and the frothy blood that dribbled from the twisted lips, she turned away quickly.

The gruesomely scarred lips moved and a voice as from out of a barrel graveled, "If that devil stallion hadn't been after my mare, you'd . . . you'd be dead this time!"

Gabe stared into the glazing eyes. "You're also the man that killed Sonseca, the Paiute woman? You and your partner."

"Who's gonna finish the job for me," Barling choked.
"And now that you ain't got any horses . . ."

Whatever the man was going to say was cut off by a
strangling sound deep in his throat. His boots thumped
hard on the dirt and his arms waved as he tried to grab
his crushed neck as if that might enable him to breathe
freely once again.

Gabe stood up and watched the killer until he shuddered
and died in agony, then he went over to Polly. "We got
two choices. We can wait by the rails until the train comes
through in a couple of days, or we can try and catch that
stud and his bay mare."

"If we wait, I've lost the ranch. I've lost everything.
But how . . ."

"I don't know," he said. "The mare is a saddlehorse
and if we can get close to her before she starts thinking
about being wild, then she'll come right up like a pet."

"And what about Diablo? You saw what he did to that
man. It was horrible."

"Once again, that stallion may have saved our lives,"
Gabe said. "It has great power. You may call it Indian
superstition, but I believe that horse was delivered here by
the Great Spirit to help us."

"How could I argue that?" Polly asked. "Especially
after what has happened this far."

Gabe looked at the dead man and then went over and
retrieved his Stetson, which now had a big hole in it. Taking one last look at the dead man, he said to himself,
"That one was good, very good. But also very unlucky."

He led Polly up the arroyo, and when they came around
a high-walled corner he saw that Diablo was oblivious of
the fact that he was trapped in a box because he was en-
ergetically breeding the tall bay mare.

The powerful stallion's forelegs were locked alongside
the dead man's stirrups, and Diablo's head seemed to be

resting on the saddle horn as his muscular haunches pistoned his arm-length and slightly bowed member in and out of the mare. The mare's legs were braced wide to support Diablo's huge weight. She stood perfectly still with her ears forward and her eyes dilated.

"This is the time to grab his reins," Polly said urgently.

"Are you kidding? That stallion and I are just starting to like each other. If I interrupted this, he'd find a way to stomp me, too."

"Then we're just going to stand here and watch?"

"Yeah," Gabe said. "Maybe we can learn something."

Polly's mouth twisted into an amused smile but she did not take her eyes off the coupling animals. "I don't think so," she said. "But I would think that the size of that stud would leave a mortal man feeling a little inadequate."

"Not me," Gabe said with a grin. "It's all a matter of how you use what you got."

Polly dabbed at his bullet-grazed scalp and then, as if unable to resist some powerful inner impulse, she kissed Gabe on the mouth and held him very close, pressing her round little hips against his. "Let's catch the horses the moment they're finished and then let's show them a thing or two."

"Here? What about . . ."

She swallowed and took his hand and placed it inside her shirt and worked it under her bra. Her breast was the softest thing in the world against his rough, calloused hand as she said, "What difference is one hour going to make?"

Gabe watched the stallion's huge member work in and out of the good-looking bay mare. "An hour won't make a damn bit of difference," he said as Diablo grunted and his massive body quivered and stiffened with fulfillment. "Not any difference at all."

CHAPTER SIXTEEN

Maybe it was crazy to make love in a brushy ravine out in the middle of the Nevada desert, but both Gabe and Polly were so hungry for each other that they could not wait another hour. The sight of the stallion and the mare coupling had fired their desire, a desire that had been building for years but which had never been acknowledged because of poor Chris.

Now, the stallion and the mare were finished and both were tied and watching as Long Rider spread his woolly haired buffalo robe on the hard ground and pulled off his clothes to stand hard and lean before Polly Benton.

Polly studied him for a long moment with hunger and then she hurriedly finished undressing. "I think I've always wanted you," she confessed. "I know this sounds terrible, but sometimes when Chris made love to me, I used to imagine it was you."

"He would have found that amusing."

"I didn't," Polly said. "I found it very, very . . . stimulating."

Gabe took the woman into his arms. Diablo nickered excitedly and Gabe said, "The stallion, look at him. He knows."

"So does the mare," Polly said, her hips beginning to twitch and move against his with anticipation.

Gabe reached down with both hands and cupped her hard buttocks and pulled her hard against his stiff manhood. She sighed and then moaned when his mouth found her lush breasts. He could feel her legs quivering as if she were a young foal trying to stand.

He lowered her to the buffalo robe and they kissed, tongues and mouths probing and hungry. Polly reached down and her small hand found his big shaft and she pulled and caressed it with increasing urgency.

"Don't play with me, Gabe. Just make love to me," she breathed in his ear.

Gabe was more than happy to do just that. He pulled away from her for a moment and watched as she opened her legs wide. He wondered if such a girlish body could hold him without pain and, even as he worried about this, she guided his throbbing shaft to the lips of her moist womanhood. She rubbed him up and down for almost a minute against her lips until she was so wet that their faint union made a sipping sound.

"It's ready now, so come on," she panted.

They both watched as Gabe rotated his hips forward and the immense head of his penis pushed its way into her eager body. "It's going," he said, a little surprised that it seemed to cause her no visible discomfort.

Polly fell back. Her breasts were rising and falling as if she were already out of breath. She stared up at the blue sky and there was a look of sheer rapture on her face. "Oh, boy, is it going!"

Gabe chuckled to see how much she was already enjoying him inside of her. He thrust his manhood even deeper and she gasped. Her knees came up and her smooth, slender thighs gripped him as solidly as Diablo's mighty forelegs had gripped the tall bay mare.

"Come on," she begged, "put it in all the way."

He licked her full breasts and rocked his hips hard against hers, pinning her to the earth and feeling her body swell up to enfold him. For a moment, she did not move and he remained poised over her as they both let the sensation spiral and whirl around them.

"Oh, yes," she whispered, "this is how I dreamed making love to you would feel!"

She immediately lost all semblance of patience. Her narrow hips began to beat at him and her hot womanhood sucked and massaged his plunging staff until they both lost control and began to slam in and out of each other. There was no beauty or technique in this, no deliberate or delicate moves. It was purely animalistic and it was wonderful. Gabe's bullet-riddled and bandaged body lost all of its pain as the woman's body lifted him to the point of ecstasy.

"Now!" she cried, her hips bucking and her womanhood milking him like a thing gone crazy.

When she threw back her head and began to cry out with pleasure, Diablo stomped and fussed with his rope and Gabe's lips curled back from his teeth as his own body jackknifed into her and emptied itself of his hot seed in great, drenching torrents that seemed never to stop. He was dimly aware of her crying out under his body and then, she went limp.

He could not stop his hips from spasming for almost a minute and when he did, Polly was so limp that he had a momentary scare and wondered if he had somehow driven himself too deep and killed her.

He needn't have worried. When her breath finally returned, she reached up and pulled his head down between her lovely breasts and sighed with contentment.

"Oh," she whispered, "I thought I was going to go crazy with you. I thought my heart was going to burst and my body was coming to pieces under you."

He started to roll off of her but she suddenly clung to him. "Don't move," she pleaded. "Not yet."

Gabe obliged her. But soon, he knew that they had to leave. They still had a long way to go to get to Reno and time was running out.

Fort Deeth was one of the most miserable outposts on the frontier. It had been built to protect the overland travelers that followed the Humboldt River across the desolate interior of Nevada on their rush to the gold fields of California and, most recently, the Comstock Lode.

For the last few years, the fort's usefulness had been questioned both by the men who were unlucky enough to command it, and also by the top military leaders in Washington. However, with the Paiute uprising, everyone was glad that the fort had not been abandoned.

Gabe and Polly's arrival caused a great stir of excitement and they were rushed to the commander's office. When Major John Pinkerton had his junior officers gathered, he proclaimed, "I have purposefully refrained from asking our visitors to speak because I wanted all of you present to hear what I am sure must be very important news to us in a straightforward, firsthand account. So please, Mr. . . ."

"Gabe," he said. "And this is Mrs. Polly Benton."

"I see. Well, Mr. and Mrs. Gabe Benton, how on earth did you get here unescorted and unprotected all the way from Elko without losing your scalp?"

It was entirely natural and not a bit surprising that the major assumed they were husband and wife and, because

Polly did not correct him, neither did Gabe. "We are on our way to Reno," he said. "It is a matter of some urgency."

"My God! Why did you not wait for the train? It will be through here day after tomorrow."

"We know that," Polly said. "But we need to reach Reno first."

She did not elaborate and neither did Gabe, who said, "We were followed by a tall man with knife scars on his face. He tried to ambush and kill us. He, along with the immigrants who are destroying the pinion pines which feed the Paiutes, are responsible for starting the Paiute uprising."

Pinkerton looked genuinely confused by this explanation. "I'm afraid I don't understand."

"It is a matter of survival for the Paiute. Apparently, their main food source is the pine nut harvest. They want the pinion pine forests to be left alone. Too many are being cut down for firewood and underground mine timbering. The Paiutes are alarmed and want those trees protected."

The major glanced at his officers. "This doesn't seem like an unreasonable request. When salted and roasted, the pine nuts are delicious. In fact, the Paiute taught us to eat and appreciate them."

"You took their lesson too seriously," Gabe said. "Indians are a generous people—until they are faced with extinction. But I think most of all, the trouble was caused by two killers who passed through this country and found a young Paiute woman named Sonseca. They raped and murdered her."

"How do you know this isn't just some excuse for the Paiute to go on the warpath?" a skeptical lieutenant blurted.

Polly's cheeks flamed. "He knows because Gabe killed

one of the men who did it. And if you can get to the body and return it to Chief Spotted Horse with both your sincere apologies and a pledge that the other man will be punished, then the rampaging will stop and peace will return to this country.''

Major Pinkerton's eyebrows raised in question. He was an intelligent-looking man with a round face and wide-spaced brown eyes. ''How are we supposed to keep such a promise when this . . . this second villain is unknown to us?''

''The chief has a button torn from the second murderer's coat. It did not belong to the big knife fighter that I shot, so it has to be his partner's. Find that coat and we will find the man.''

''Easier to find the proverbial needle in the haystack,'' another officer said. ''This is a big country.''

''I know that,'' Gabe answered. ''But I have a hunch that the man who can end this trouble is coming after me. I think we will meet in Reno.''

The officers looked at each other and it was clear they were confused and skeptical. However, the major said, ''Anything you can do on your part to end the bloodshed and this war will be greatly appreciated. The sooner this is settled, the sooner I can get off a report to Washington and recommend that this fort be abandoned or at least replaced. This, as you can see, is a hellish existence.''

Now Gabe understood why the commander of Fort Deeth was being so cooperative. ''Do you have a map?''

''Why, of course.''

''Bring it out, please. I will show you where the body of the man is and in which direction you should take it. Chief Spotted Horse speaks good English, as does his son, Temesca.''

Pinkerton nodded. ''I know them well. They are both intelligent and educated men. Before this outbreak of hostilities, they frequently visited this fort. They have, in fact, spent time in this very room.''

"Then you must realize what a violent provocation it took to start this war,'' Polly said. ''And that you have the opportunity to end it.''

"Yes,'' the major said. ''And you be sure that I will if it is within my power. However, this other vicious killer . . . how . . .''

"Tell the chief I am hunting for him,'' Gabe interrupted. ''And that I will bring the man's head back to him in my saddlebag.''

Major Pinkerton opened his mouth to object, then he looked deep into Gabe's eyes and changed his mind. ''Very well,'' he said, glancing at his equally shocked officers. ''That comment of yours is taken off the record. The civil authorities would not approve, and neither do I. We would prefer that you bring the suspect back alive.''

"For what!'' Gabe snapped. ''To see him go to trial and then set free for lack of evidence? You know that a lost button won't convict him. No, the only way justice can be meted out is to do it myself.''

Gabe took Polly's arm. He bowed slightly to the major and then said, ''We are in a horse race, gentlemen. I hope you understand that.''

The major nodded. They walked outside and then a corporal came running up to them. ''Sir!'' he cried. ''There is a little problem down at stables.''

"What problem?'' the major demanded.

"It's this man's Appaloosa stallion, Major. He broke out of that corral and got into our big one. He's . . .'' The corporal stammered.

"Out with it!'' the major shouted.

The corporal's cheeks were red as he said, ''Well, sir, he's breeding a couple of our mares and nobody can get near him.''

The major's eyes widened and he looked at Gabe. "Mr. Benton, kindly get that big stallion the hell out of Fort Deeth before I have it shot or castrated!"

"I'll do it," Gabe said, trying to hide a smile as he took Polly's arm and started for the corrals, where dust was rising and soldiers were gathered to watch the stallion take his lusty pleasure.

Once again, Gabe showed the good sense to wait until Diablo had finished his business. It was clear that the stallion wanted to drive the army mares out of the fort and off to some faraway range where he could return to the lordship that he had always known.

"Be patient," Gabe said to the Appaloosa when the breeding was done and he managed to get a rope around Diablo's head. "Good things come to those who wait."

"The hell they do," Polly whispered. "And I don't think you believe that for a minute."

"No," Gabe admitted as he bridled the stallion, who, for the moment at least, seemed content. "But it was all I could think of to say."

The soldiers saddled the bay mare for Polly, almost fighting over the honor of doing it for her. Then she and Long Rider waved farewell as Major Pinkerton formed a patrol to find the body and deliver it to Chief Spotted Horse before there was any more trouble.

As they rode west, swinging fast through the brush, Gabe had a good feeling that things were finally starting to turn in their favor. All he had to do now was to get to Reno before the news of the Frontier Bank failure arrived on the train. That, and find the second killer and maybe even the corrupt banker from Ogden.

CHAPTER SEVENTEEN

Dalton Kimbal heard the Union Pacific locomotive's shrill steam whistle as it pulled into the Elko train station. He grabbed his valise and suitcase, then departed his miserable hotel room with more than a little relief. On his way out, he locked the door, then slipped the key halfway under it so that it could be retrieved. He was excited to finally be on his way.

Two doors down, he rapped smartly on Curly Cutter's door. "Open up!" he called. "The train only stops for thirty minutes."

"I'll meet you at the station," Curly said in a thick voice.

"Like hell you will!" Kimbal swore. "I'm paying you to protect me, goddamn it! Open up!"

Kimbal heard Curly swear and then a moment later, the door opened. Curly was as naked as the day he was born and his eyes were bright and his face flushed. Kimbal hardly noticed because the man's most prominent feature was his huge, wet erection.

Kimbal leaped back into the hallway. "What's the matter with you!" he cried.

"Ain't a damn thing the matter with me that another minute with Mona won't fix," Curly said breathlessly.

Mona giggled and winked at Kimbal, who stared at her.

Curly sneered at the banker. "Mr. Kimbal, you sure know how to time things bad," he said, jerking his thumb over his shoulder at the prostitute that was sitting up in Curly's bed wearing nothing but a loose smile and her costume jewelry.

"Get rid of her and let's go!" the banker hissed, coming inside. He looked at the woman with disgust. "You get out of here—now!"

"What's the big hurry?" Mona pouted. In her prime, she had been a looker, but now pushing forty and hard used, she had dyed red hair and puffy eyes. Her breasts rode her chest like a pair of empty saddlebags and Kimbal could smell her sweat, which made him feel a little ill.

He pulled out his wallet and peeled off ten dollars. "Just get out of here and don't come back."

She produced a pint of whiskey from under the pillow and smiled. "So you're Curly's sugar daddy," she said, taking a long drink. "Why don't you cash that ten dollars on the best screwin' you ever had in your life?"

Kimbal's cheeks flamed. He spun around to face Curly, who was grinning stupidly, and yelled in the gunman's face. "I want her out of here in sixty goddamn seconds or you're fired."

Curly's grin died and he screeched, "You just try to fire me, Mr. Kimbal! You do that and I'll tell everyone about that Ogden bank you . . ."

Kimbal lost control. He reached for his derringer, but Curly chopped his wrist and knocked the little pistol flying. "I ought to kill you and take what's in that valise and be done with this!" Curly spat.

Kimbal looked into the man's eyes and he swallowed loudly. "Listen," he said. "Let's just get out of this town. You still got a lot more money coming in Reno. There's no sense in us having a falling out! Not when we're finally able to leave this hellhole."

Curly wiped his lips. He looked over at the prostitute, then back at Kimbal. "I need another minute or two," he said doggedly. "That's all I need and that's what I'm taking."

Kimbal wanted to scream in frustration. He knew full well that if he left the man, Curly would screw himself into missing the train. But given the man's truculence and refusal to leave until he'd satisfied his lust, Kimbal knew he would be forced to endure hearing them rut. Neither choice was to his liking, but because he was afraid to go to the train station without protection, he opted to remain with Curly.

"Oh, go ahead, then. But make it fast."

Curly chuckled. "I'm already halfway to heaven," he said, turning away and bounding toward the bed as Kimbal crossed the room to retrieve his derringer.

Kimbal saw the prostitute open her legs, take another pull on the whiskey, and then grunt as Curly actually jumped and impaled her with his rod. The banker closed his eyes and heard their bodies slapping wetly and the sound of the protesting bedsprings. Almost at once, the prostitute began to make a low, groaning sound, and Kimbal hated himself because he could not help but watch.

Kimbal was not a virgin. He had had women, but not many and not for a long, long time. Now, as he peeped through his squinted eyes, he was ashamed at his own powerful and unexpected feeling of raw desire. He felt his member swelling and pushing strongly at his underclothes, and he was filled with shame and certain that Curly would notice his erection and make a big joke out of it.

Still, despite all his embarrassment and shame, the banker stared with sensual fascination at the pair of wildly rutting bodies. It truly amazed him how energetic and athletic sex could be among younger, very healthy and earthy types. The few times that he had known a woman, sex had been a ginger and almost tentative adventure, and Kimbal had always washed himself immediately after intercourse as if he could wash away a feeling of sinfulness.

But these two coupled with the pure animal abandonment of a couple of dogs in the street. The prostitute was giving at least as good as she was getting, and though it might be an act on her part, it seemed to Kimbal that she was having a thrilling time while earning her money. No woman that he had ever lain beside had shown as much excitement as Mona now exhibited.

"Oh, Curly!" the prostitute cried. "Yes. Yes!"

Kimbal's eyes widened as he saw the woman's flaccid white body start bucking and her legs flap like fast-beating wings. He heard her pure animal cry of ecstasy and then saw Curly's lean hips piston in and out and then convulse.

Kimbal swallowed dryly. He moaned low in his own throat, then turned quickly toward the wall, horrified to realize he was also having an orgasm. He almost died of shame and had to steady himself against the wall for support as his skinny legs trembled. He was depraved!

"Hurry and get dressed," he panted, discovering his breath was tight and short. "I can't miss that train!"

"Hold on to your cock and we'll be out of here in two minutes!" Curly sang as he jumped out of bed, grabbed his pants, and then dressed with an amazing economy of motion. He smoothed his long, wavy black hair with his fingers, strapped on his six-gun, and then kissed Mona good-bye before grabbing his own war bag of gear.

"You can turn around now, Mr. Kimbal. Ain't nothing going on that would offend a man like you anymore."

"Let's go," Kimbal said, not about to turn around and much too embarrassed to look down at his heavy wool trousers and see if there was a wet spot that would betray his own wicked desire.

Before Curly could think of anything else to say, Kimbal hurried out the door and down the hallway, which was mercifully dim. The banker went down the back steps and out into the alley.

"You stay close and watch for trouble!" he cried. "There might be someone from Ogden on board."

"If there is, they better keep their mouth shut or I'll kill 'em for sure."

When the banker reached the train station, he was practically running but saw at once that there were no passengers out on the loading platform and that it was unlikely he would meet anyone who knew him if he kept his guard up until the train arrived in Reno.

"All aboard!" the black porter called. "All aboard whose gettin' on board."

Kimbal shoved the ticket he had bought days ago at the man and rushed past him before he could notice the wet spot on his pants.

"You got berth twenty-two!" the porter called.

Kimbal shot into the train and found his berth very quickly. He jumped inside and pulled the curtain shut behind him.

"Mr. Kimbal?" Curly asked, not pulling the curtain open but standing in the narrow passageway.

"What do you want now?"

"I just wanted to say that I've got the berth right across the passageway from you. If there's any trouble, they'll have to come past me."

"Good! Now leave me alone."

There was a moment of silence and then Curly sounded hurt when he said, "We're supposed to be in Reno tomorrow about noon. I'll not sleep until then, so don't worry about that part of it.''

"I won't,''. the banker said, unbuttoning his trousers almost in a wild panic to rid himself of them.

The train jerked him nearly off his feet. He bounced against the wall of his berth and almost toppled out half-naked into the passageway as the train began to roll westward.

Kimbal reached into his suitcase and found a fresh and clean pair of undershorts and trousers. With a grimace of disgust on his face, he hurriedly undressed, pulled on his fresh underwear, then wadded up the soiled evidence of his own lust. He leaned across his berth, pulled open his window and breathed in smoke from the locomotive.

He ignored the smoke until the train was completely out of town, and then he hurled the wicked bundle out the window into the brush.

Kimbal slammed the window shut and collapsed on his bed. He closed his eyes, but almost instantly was assailed by the vision of Curly humping the prostitute. The banker's own flaccid little worm started to grow again and Kimbal groaned with despair and sat up quickly. He needed a cold bath. Yes, that was the thing!

"Porter!" he shouted, pulling his curtain open just enough to stick his face through. "Porter, I need a basin of cold water.''

"Yessuh!''

Kimbal pulled the curtain closed again and sat back down to wait. Across the passageway, he heard Curly's mocking laughter and the banker's cheeks burned with shame and his hands clenched in cold fury.

Curly knew! He knew how Kimbal had weakened with desire and succumbed to the needs of his own traitorous flesh.

The banker cupped his face in his hands and felt waves

of shame beat over him until it was replaced by hatred and loathing.

He was going to poison that man before they reached Reno.

Yes! And he would do it tonight.

"Yo water, suh!"

Kimbal pulled himself out of his reverie of revenge and opened the curtain just enough to take the basin of water. He smiled gratefully and the porter returned his smile and waited.

A tip. Yes. Kimbal hastily retreated back inside his little berth and found his wallet. He tipped the porter with a whole dollar and then he said, "What time is dinner served in the dining car?"

"Eight o'clock, suh."

"Thank you. Please reserve me a nice table."

The porter nodded and left quickly.

"Hey!" Curly said, yanking his curtain open and staring at him with accusing eyes. "What about me? I'm gonna be damned hungry, too!"

Kimbal thought about the poison. "I'll bring you back something."

"But . . ."

"I'd rather we didn't dine together."

Curly seemed to understand, or at least told himself he understood. "All right," he snapped. "But as soon as we finish our business in Reno, I want to be paid off and done with you. I'm tired of you acting like I was something lower than a damn bug. I'm as good as you are. So was Dan."

"Dan is dead," Kimbal said. "If he wasn't, he'd have returned to Elko."

"Maybe and maybe not," Curly said stubbornly. "Could be that he had to chase Long Rider most of the way to Reno and just decided to go on in."

Kimbal said nothing. He wanted Dan Barling dead and out of the way. "I'll bring you back a nice dinner," he promised.

"Ain't that the porter's job?"

Kimbal smiled. "I want to get you something real special, since you're going to stay up all night while I sleep. You're doing me a good service, Curly. I just thought that I'd show my appreciation."

The gunman was surprised and then pleased. "Well," he said, puffing up a little, "I'm glad you finally realized that."

"I have," Kimbal said, retreating back into his berth and pulling his curtain shut. "Now leave me in peace until dinnertime."

When he heard Curly's bunk squeak with protest under his weight, Kimbal took up his valise, opened it with a key, and then removed the rat poison.

He read the label very carefully and decided that it would take at least a tablespoon to kill Curly. He would have to doctor the man's food carefully. Perhaps the poison would only make Curly very ill and he would have to suffocate the man while he lay incapacitated in his berth.

Kimbal shook his head, finding the idea very unpleasant. He did not wish to physically touch Curly. The man was a degenerate of the worst order. He consorted with whores and might even have contracted the Frenchman's disease.

Better slip him two tablespoons, Kimbal decided.

CHAPTER EIGHTEEN

They had left the Humboldt River and crossed a waterless sixty-mile stretch of nothing but alkali flats and salt beds. Thankfully, it was wintertime in the desert, but Gabe and Polly could see the cast-off treasures of wagon trains that had suffered from blistering summer attempts to cross this long, arid stretch. There were stoves and broken axles, skeletons of mules and oxen, and hundreds of rusty farm implements that had been tossed aside in a desperate effort to reach the Truckee River in the years before the railroads had spanned this vast wasteland.

"There it is," Gabe said. "The Truckee. That faint blue line on the horizon is the peaks of the Sierra Nevada."

Polly studied the view for several moments. "The mountains are sure a welcome sight, but the river doesn't look like much to speak of."

"It did to the overland travelers coming across this desert," Gabe said. "Besides, the Truckee just sinks into the desert out here. As we follow it toward the Sierras, it will get bigger.''

"Look over there!" Polly said, pointing to the southwest. "Isn't that a covered wagon and a pair of horses on the ground way out in the brush?''

Gabe squinted. "You're right. And from the way it's leaning way over sideways, it looks like the wagon has broke down.''

"Maybe we'd better ride over there and make sure that whoever is in it is all right.''

"We'll be losing an hour or more," Gabe cautioned. "That wagon looks close, but it's six, maybe even seven miles out of our way. And if we have to stop and help them, then we'll lose even more time.''

"I know," Polly said. "But they're way out there by themselves and you can see they're in a bad fix. I'd not feel right if we didn't see if we could help.''

"You're the boss," Gabe said. "But that train is due to come along sometime today. If we don't get a move on, then we'll be in a fix, and you stand to lose the chance to cash that big check.''

Polly bit her lower lip nervously. She fretted over the tough decision a moment and then said, "How far to Reno now?''

"Thirty miles at least.''

"We'll just stop for a few minutes. Maybe we can cut through those mountains to the south and save a few miles.''

"Maybe," Gabe admitted. "Reno is on a more direct line that way, but this is hard country to go exploring, and we could wind up in a fix.''

"We'll just have to take that chance," Polly said. "There may be women and children in that wagon.''

"Then let's go," Gabe said, reining the Appaloosa toward the distant wagon and letting it run as Polly and the bay mare came in close to match them stride for stride.

When they grew nearer, Gabe could see that the wagon was badly mired and that one of the horses was stiff in death and the other animal looked too weak to rise. No question about it, whoever was here was in big trouble.

Gabe reined Diablo in a hundred yards from the covered wagon. "Anybody home!" he shouted.

"Help!" came a weak cry from inside the wagon.

Gabe spurred the Appaloosa on at a run, and when he reached the wagon, his keen eyes noted that the signs indicated that the wagon had been stuck for many days. The horse that was still alive was suffering some inner malady and it was groaning weakly as if it had been poisoned.

He dismounted and tied Diablo to one of the wheels and Polly tied her horse to the other. They both hurried around the wagon to look inside.

"Oh my gosh!" Polly breathed.

Gabe's face tightened. Inside the wagon was a man and a woman and they were both white as snow. A second glance revealed that the man was dead and the woman was desperately ill and extremely weak. She had to struggle just to raise her head and stare at her visitors.

"Help me, please," she whispered, tears rolling down her sunken cheeks. "I need water."

Polly was inside the wagon in a moment and Gabe snatched his canteen and followed her. "Here," he said, "drink some of this."

The woman, who was about Polly's age and size but much thinner, looked at them both with wide eyes and rasped, "Is it . . . is it *good* water?"

"Yes," Gabe said, cradling her head. "Now take a sip."

But the woman was still not convinced. "Where . . . where did the water come from?"

"From the Humboldt River," Polly said. "Please, you must drink."

The woman stared at the canteen for several seconds and there was real fear in her eyes. "Arthur and I drank poison water. And now . . . now he's . . . dead!"

"I'll bury him," Gabe said. "But you have to save yourself."

"That's right," Polly added quickly. "Won't you please drink? Arthur would want you to live."

The woman blinked and then dipped her chin. "Yes," she said quietly and with great deliberation. "He would. He'd want me to live. He told me that before he died. He said . . ."

Gabe pushed the mouth of his canteen to her cracked lips. The woman took a sip, then a swallow, and then she grabbed the canteen with fingers like talons and started to gulp. Gabe pulled the canteen back.

"You have to take it slow at first," he said. "I'm sorry, but it's the best way."

The woman looked up at them. "Who are you?" she whispered.

"We're friends," Polly said. "We're going to get you out of here. We'll take you to Reno."

"But that's where we came from! Arthur and I were going to Austin. To the gold strike. We were taking a shortcut. They said that all the good claims were being gobbled up so fast that we'd get nothing if we went on the freight road."

Gabe gave her another drink and she continued. "We heard about the Paiutes on the warpath, but had to take the chance and come out alone this way."

"Arthur's dead and so are your horses," Gabe said. "At least, one of them is dead and the other is dying. I'll have to shoot it, ma'am. It's suffering."

"Yes, yes, I could hear the poor beast struggling to

breathe and to get up. Arthur wanted so badly to put it out of its misery. He was kind toward animals. He was a very kind man.''

But a stupid one, Gabe thought. A stupid one to have struck out across uninhabited country and gotten himself bogged down in deep sand and then to have found some contaminated source of water instead of riding back to the Truckee River.

"I'll get her ready," Polly said. "You tend to things outside."

"She's not strong enough to ride without me holding her up in front of me or else making a travois."

"Do what you think is best."

Gabe backed out of the wagon. The first thing he did was to walk over to the dying horse. He wore his six-gun on his right side, butt forward, and because of his bent index finger, he favored the cross draw using his left hand. Pulling the big Colt out of its holster, Gabe shot the suffering horse behind the ear.

It quivered and its agony was finally over. Gabe studied the ground and read the struggle that had taken place here. He could see where the man had tried to use planks and boards off his own wagon to shove under the sunken wheels and free himself from the sand. But with two dying horses and fire in his own guts, it must have been obvious even to Arthur that he was beaten.

Gabe decided against a travois. They worked well on the northern plains, where he was raised, but out here in this heavily brush- and rock-strewn country, a travois would not hold together more than a few miles and its occupant would be badly shaken.

"How's it going in there?" he called.

"You can come inside for Arthur," Polly said in a low voice.

The woman sobbed and began to cry. Gabe crawled

back inside the wagon and struggled to pull the dead man out as quickly as possible.

Arthur had been a handsome man but one much too slight of build to have braved this rough country. Even in his prime, he could not have weighed over 140 pounds, and would have stood maybe five eight. Gabe gently removed him from the wagon and carried him out of the sand to a place where the ground was harder. He found a pick and shovel and went right to work digging a grave.

The ground was thick with rocks and it took Gabe nearly two hours to slash a proper grave and then get the man buried. He kept looking up at the sun and wishing they could get riding because that train was going to come along at any time.

To the north, the shining rails of the transcontinental railroad could be seen and Gabe knew that time was running out for Polly Benton. If the train reached Reno before they did with the news of the Frontier Bank's failure, that twelve-thousand-dollar check that Dalton Kimbal had issued would be worthless.

"Please," the woman whose name was Hester said. "Can I just be with Arthur a few minutes in prayer before we go?"

"Of course you can," Polly said, looking at Gabe, who lifted the woman in his strong arms. "Take all the time you need."

Hester weighed practically nothing and Gabe sat her down on a blanket beside the grave, then he and Polly left her to be alone.

"What time would you say it was?" Polly asked, glancing up at the sun.

"About eleven o'clock. What time does the train arrive in Reno?"

"At four," Polly said.

"We won't beat the train carrying her," Gabe said quietly. "Not even close."

"I know that," Polly said. "You'll have to stay with her and let me go on ahead."

"What?"

"It's my only hope. I'm not strong enough to hold that woman up and you can't cash the check because it's made out to me."

Gabe shook his head violently. "But there may be trouble waiting for you in Reno!"

"I know what Mr. Kimbal looks like and I also have a pretty fair idea of what that other gunman that attacked and almost killed us in Elko looks like. I carry a gun and I'll just have to take my chances. It's either that or lose everything. I have to go on alone, Gabe."

He knew Polly was right, though he hated like the devil to admit it. Gabe chewed it around several times in his mind and the solution always came up the same. Polly would have to go on the last thirty miles alone, and even on her bay mare she'd be cutting things mighty fine.

Dammit! Gabe thought. The bitter reality was that they could not leave the sick woman behind and they could not get to Reno with her before the train arrived. It was a bad situation. One that Gabe had never expected.

"Then you'd better get going," he said. "I'll be in before midnight. There's a hotel called the Washoe on Virginia Street. That's where I'll look for you."

"I'll be waiting."

Polly reached over and hugged his neck. "This is going to be much harder on you than it is on me. I'll be all right. Just get that poor, sick woman to a doctor before you come for me."

"I will," he promised. "And when you cash that check, go down the street and put it into another bank first thing.

One that looks substantial and in no danger of folding. And, Polly?''

''Yes?''

Gabe pointed northwest toward Reno. ''You're going to have to try to find a shortcut.''

''I'll find one.''

Gabe watched Polly go over to Hester. He heard her tell the widow that she had to hurry off but that Gabe would take care of her and bring her into Reno.

''We'll find you help and a room,'' she promised. ''Tomorrow morning, I'll have a wonderful breakfast brought up to your room and we'll talk. You'll feel much, much better.''

''I can't thank you enough,'' Hester said. ''You and your friend have saved my life. I wish you didn't have to go.''

''I have to,'' Polly said. ''My ranch depends on it. You see, I also lost my husband. And maybe . . . well, maybe we can become friends and help each other.''

Gabe watched Polly remount the tall bay. She waved a grim good-bye and then took off at a hard gallop heading straight toward a cut in the rugged hills. Right now the bay mare was sailing but Gabe knew that the terrain was going to get rougher before it got better.

He turned and saw that Hester had returned her attention to the grave and her lips were moving in prayer.

Gabe settled back on his haunches and waited patiently. Time was no longer a critical factor. It was all up to Polly and the bay mare.

CHAPTER NINETEEN

Dalton Kimbal slipped rat poison into the soup and the coffee before he tipped a porter to deliver it to Curly Cutter in Berth 23. Not wishing to be conspicuous, he kept his face averted toward the window during his own meal, and when darkness fell and he could see the stars over the desert, he remained in his seat until the porter returned.

"Did you deliver Mr. Cutter's tray without any difficulty?" he asked.

"Oh, yessuh," the black porter said. "Mr. Cutter, he say he real hungry."

"Excellent!" Kimbal could scarcely contain his joy. "And now, a Cuban cigar and a bottle of your best champagne, if you please!"

The porter grinned. "You havin' a little celebration, suh?"

"I am," Kimbal replied. "And if you hurry, I will tip you another dollar."

The porter's eyes grew round with delight. "Yessuh!"

The banker had his cigar and sipped his champagne

until the hour grew very late and he became tipsy and sleepy. He pulled out his pocket watch and noted that it was three minutes past midnight.

"Porter," he said in a slow, deliberate voice designed not to reveal the effect the champagne was having. "Are there any towns out here?"

"Oh, no suh! Not unless you mean prairie dog towns!"

The porter chuckled at his own joke and, because of the champagne, Kimbal laughed a bit too loud. But it was all in good fun and there was no harm done or intended. Black people were humans, after all, though this one did seem to be a little too familiar. But at least, he thought, I can toss Cutter's body out and it will not be found for days.

Kimbal climbed a trifle unsteadily to his feet and managed to make a decent exit of the dining car. He careened down the aisle to a sleeping car and when he reached Cutter's berth, he steeled himself to witness the ghastly sight of a man locked in the agonies of death by poisoning.

Instead, when he struck a match and pulled the curtains open, he found Cutter fast asleep, with his mouth wide open and a very peaceful look on his face.

"Dammit!" Kimbal swore, grabbing the man and jerking him into wakefulness. "Dammit, man, what are you doing asleep?"

"Huh," Cutter said groggily.

"I said, what are you doing asleep?"

Cutter roused himself slowly. He knuckled his eye sockets and sat up, expelling a big yawn. "Sorry about that, Mr. Kimbal," he said, stifling another yawn. "I know I said I'd stay awake all night, but the rocking of this train put me under, and I had a little drink of whiskey before that dinner you sent. I just fell asleep on a full stomach."

Kimbal glanced down at the floor and now he saw the tray he'd sent by porter shoved halfway under the berth.

He could not help but pull it out. "You didn't drink your coffee or taste your soup?"

"I hate pea soup," Cutter said almost apologetically. "And like I said, I was drinking a little whiskey. Just a couple of snorts, mind you. I ain't too drunk to protect you. Say, you look a little drunk yourself."

Kimbal bristled with righteous outrage. "I am nothing of the sort!"

"It's all right." Cutter grinned. "I still got a little whiskey if you want to share a nip."

"I do not!"

"Suit yourself," Cutter said with a lazy shrug of his shoulders. "But no more for me, either. I'm staying right here and awake all night long. That little nap did it for me. That, and screwing Mona. Be honest. Wouldn't you have liked to have had a little of that yourself? Come on and admit it, Mr. Kimbal! She really knows how to work a man down to a nubbin, doesn't she."

Kimbal's cheeks flushed with shame. "Good night, Mr. Cutter!"

"Night," the man said, dropping to his feet and stretching. "Tomorrow is the big payday that Dan Barling and I waited for. I know it means more for me this way, but I still wish he'd have made it. Old Dan and I, we went through some whiskey and women. Why, I remember the time that . . ."

The banker was so furious that he almost lost his head and struck the man in the face. But he was not quite that drunk and so he slammed into his berth and yanked the curtain shut.

Dammit anyway! Now he would have to wait until breakfast to attempt to poison that fool again.

He missed another chance to do it at breakfast because he was so hung over from the bottle of champagne that he overslept, and in the morning his head was so bad that he could not bear to get up and get moving.

Kimbal felt awful and went back to sleep for a few minutes—or so he intended. Actually, by the time he awoke, it was midafternoon and the train was following the Truckee River into Reno.

With a groan, he exited his berth and found the lavatory to wash his face, shave, and try to pull his jangled nerves and shattered mind into one functioning unit.

By the time the train was rolling into Reno, he had managed to calm his queasy stomach and prepare himself adequately for what he had to do next.

"I need to get to the Frontier Bank before it closes," he told a grinning Curly Cutter. "Hail us transportation while I gather my things. Hurry, man!"

Curly did not like to hurry and he liked even less taking orders. Still, it was payday and he was determined not to get into a fight with Kimbal until after he had been paid and could think of a way to kill the banker and steal what he was sure would be a small fortune.

Curly had speculated all the previous night on how much money Kimbal would be taking out of the Frontier Bank. He had finally settled on a figure. A nice, big fat figure of a hundred thousand dollars. That might be on the high side, but anything over fifty was a small fortune.

Curly practically threw another couple of train passenger off the only for-hire surry that was waiting at the train depot.

"Sorry, folks," he said to the other couple as he took their place in the seat behind the driver, "but tough luck. Me and my friend are in a big hurry."

"Well, so are we!" the angry man who had first claim on the surry exclaimed. "And I demand that you vacate that vehicle at once."

"Yes, out at once!" the woman demanded, stamping her foot.

Curly grinned maliciously. The woman was not bad looking. A little fat, but Curly liked fat women. A little old, but Curly had discovered that older women were often more skilled in bed.

"Did you hear me, you grinning jackass!" the man yelled.

Curly turned away from admiring the woman and fantasizing about making love to her and he drew his six-gun and pointed it at the man. "Are you in a hurry to die, big mouth?"

The woman screamed and the man's jaw dropped and he began to quake as he stared at the pistol so rock steady in Curly's hand. "Oh, no, sir! Take the surry. It's all yours, sir!"

"Thanks," Curly said with a triumphant grin. "I thought you might have a change of heart."

"What's the problem here?" Kimbal said, rushing up.

Curly turned his pistol in the driver's general direction. "Not a thing, is there, driver?"

"Oh, no, sir!" the driver stammered. He jumped out of the cab and grabbed the suitcase from Kimbal's hand. "Hop right in, sir. Where would you like to go?"

"Frontier Bank on Virginia Street. And hurry! I need to do business before closing time."

Kimbal looked at his watch. It was four-twenty. He would be inside the bank by four-thirty and it was open until five. He had made it! The telegraph wires were still down and there was no way that the banking officials here would know of his Ogden bank's failure. Oh, sure, they'd have a few questions, but nothing that he couldn't bluff his way through as he cashed the checks in his valise and then strolled out the door.

• • •

The instant the surry rolled up to the bank, Kimbal
leaped out, paid the driver, and said, "Curly, you stay
right here just in case you see someone familiar."

"Ain't much chance of that," Curly said. "No way
anybody could beat us here."

"You never know," Kimbal said. He smoothed his coat,
straightened his tie, and moved quickly toward the bank.
He stepped inside and then saw Polly Benton. She was
smiling and getting ready to turn away from the cashier
and Kimbal heard her say to the cashier, "Thank you for
the cash. I know this probably puts a strain on your bank,
but I had to have cash."

"It's quite all right," the bank teller said, clearly worried. "It's just that you shouldn't carry such a large sum.
Anything could happen out there."

"I'll be all right," Polly said.

Kimbal slipped back out the door a moment before Polly
turned to leave. Curly was standing close to the door and
the surry was already rolling down Virginia Street south
toward the Truckee River Bridge.

"What's wrong!" Curly said when he saw the banker's
face.

"It's Polly Benton!" he breathed. "She's here and she
cashed her check for twelve thousand dollars. It's impossible she could have gotten here before us but . . . dammit, she *is* here!"

At just that moment, Polly reached the door and Kimbal
twisted around so that his back was toward her and Curly
did the same. Polly, her mind on the cash in her purse,
hurried past them and started down the street toward the
Bank of Nevada. Her money would be safe there.

"Don't do a thing," Kimbal hissed, falling in behind
her and jamming his derringer into Polly's backbone, "except exactly what you are told! Do you understand?"

Polly almost fainted. She caught the sight of the corrupt

Ogden banker, but just when she decided to scream for help, Curly drew his gun and bashed her alongside the head, then caught her before she could drop.

"Into the alley!" Kimbal whispered, helping to support the woman so that it looked as if she were being escorted rather than being carried.

They dragged Polly into the alley and Kimbal dropped her and riffled her purse for the big roll of cash. "Check to see if anyone saw us," Kimbal said.

Curly jumped back to the street, looked both ways, and said, "Nope."

Kimbal's mind raced as he stared at the unconscious woman. "Hide her," he said. "I've got to get back inside that bank and cash my own checks. By tomorrow morning it will be too late. The news of my bank's collapse will have gotten to them and the checks I carry will be worthless."

Curly, usually calm and assured, now seemed a little rattled. "Well, where do I take her?"

"I don't give a damn. Just find a place. Anyplace you won't be seen."

"No," Curly said, coming to a decision. "I'll gag her and keep her right here until you come out of that bank with all the money. Then, we can both decide what to do with her."

Kimbal didn't like that idea at all, but he could see that Curly wasn't budging and his mind was made up and would not be changed.

Kimbal was desperate to rid himself of Curly and the woman. "What if I give you five thousand dollars, right now, to get rid of her."

"Uh-uh," Curly said. "Not when you just took a hell of a lot more than that off her and plan to get another hundred thousand in cold cash."

"A hundred thousand! Are you crazy?"

"We're waiting right here," Curly said, turning his gun on the banker. "And just to make sure you come back, you're going to hand over all that money you just took out of her purse. Now!"

Kimbal swallowed. He'd be willing to give Curly the twelve thousand to get rid of him and the girl—if he could have trusted the gunman to keep his word. But Curly *wouldn't* keep his word. He'd take the twelve thousand and then he'd try to figure out a way to get all the rest. He'd wait in ambush, and odds were, Kimbal would not live to see the light of another new day.

Better to go along with the man and at least know where he was than to die with a bullet or a knife in the back. "All right," he said, handing the money over to Curly. "But no double crosses. Understood?"

"Why, sure!" Curly grinned hugely. "We keep things clean between us and we both live to be rich. That's fine with me. I ain't greedy."

The hell you aren't, Kimbal thought.

"Fair enough," Kimbal said. "Wait here and I'll be right back."

"Don't get lost," Curly said, holstering his six-gun. "Me and the little woman will be waiting. I guess she and I can find some way to amuse me."

"She's unconscious, you animal! Leave her alone!"

"Git!" Curly spat.

Kimbal left quickly and he was not sure that, once he had the checks cashed, he would dare to go back into the alley with Curly Cutter. In fact, he decided before he re-entered the bank that the best thing for him to do would be to take the money and run.

CHAPTER TWENTY

Kimbal's insides were quaking as he reentered the Reno branch of the Frontier Bank. But he had been in tough situations before and was able to assume an expression of confidence as he strode across the lobby and stopped before the cashier, who was counting his daily cash receipts in preparation of ending another business day. From all appearances, the cashier and one other employer were the only ones left to close the bank. The manager had left early. Splendid! The young cashier would remember him from a previous visit.

"Umm humm!" Kimbal cleared his throat with authority. The young cashier who had just helped Polly Benton looked up suddenly. "Mr. Kimbal! Why, how are you, sir!"

"In a hurry, I'm afraid," Kimbal said without warmth. "I'm just passing through Reno and I must catch the next train back to Ogden. I've got a few checks with me that I need to cash. I assume your bank manager and my friend, Mr. Smithers, has informed you of this."

The cashier looked confused. "Why, no, sir. And he's gone for the day."

"No matter," Kimbal said, pulling a stack of checks out of the inside of his coat pocket. "These checks are made out to our bank and total $27,289.91. I need them cashed before I board the train."

The cashier blinked and his hands began to tremble ever so slightly. Kimbal pretended not to notice as he impatiently yanked his pocket watch from his vest. "Hurry, hurry! My train returns to Ogden in less than forty minutes!"

"But . . . but, Mr. Kimbal, I don't have anywhere near that much cash."

"Let me speak to your superior," Kimbal stormed.

"That would be Mr. Isley. He's new here, sir."

The cashier frantically signaled the man over. Isley was foppish and in his early thirties. His hair was slicked down with brilliantine and parted in the middle. He wore gold-rimmed spectacles and his hands were long and pretty. He listened to the cashier's explanation and when he spoke, his voice was girlish and ingratiating.

"Mr. Kimbal, what an honor to finally meet you! I've not been here long, but my professional banking experience is considerable, and I wish that I could assist you, but we really are low on cash at the moment. You see, we just had a lady in who cashed a check for twelve thousand dollars."

"That's not my concern," Kimbal said with mounting exasperation. "As you can see, those checks are made out to our bank, and I'm going to be greatly embarrassed if they can't be cashed."

"Oh, but they can!" Isley smiled nervously and wrung his skinny hands. "It's just that it's too late in the day to borrow cash from another bank. But if you came back tomorrow, we could honor those checks by noon."

"I already explained that I've got to catch a train out in forty . . . no, thirty-six minutes!"

Isley's smiled slipped and sweat popped out across his brow. "Sir," he pleaded, "you're a banker, you must understand the predicament that you've just placed us in. If we'd had some warning . . ."

"A good bank shouldn't need any warning!" Kimbal shouted. "How much cash do you have in the vault right now?"

"Only about sixteen thousand."

"I'll take it and you can wire the rest to Ogden. Have it ready and waiting when I arrive. Do you understand me, Mr. Isley?"

"Of course!" Isley almost grabbed his hand and kissed it he was so relieved. "And thank you for being so very, very understanding."

"Just get the cash, and hurry," Kimbal snapped, scribbling his endorsements on the checks and shoving them rudely across the counter to the cashier and adding, "I'll want receipts for the checks that I'm not receiving in cash."

"Of course, sir!"

Kimbal turned his back on the pair and waited, making a big show of consulting his impressive gold pocket watch every minute or two.

He could hear the two bank employees scrambling frantically to get the cash out of the vault and to count it and take care of the necessary disbursement paperwork.

Kimbal began to pace back and forth. Sixteen thousand dollars. Much better than prison. Not a fortune, but a significant amount of cash. It was not difficult to resign himself to this outcome, which now forced him to take this lesser sum and take flight, leaving Cutter with twelve thousand for himself along with the knotty problem of how to dispose of the Benton woman.

Tomorrow or the next day for certain, news would arrive from Ogden that his bank had failed. It would cause a panic here and he'd be the object of an immediate and extensive manhunt. But no matter. He was taking the train to Sacramento. From there, he would go to San Francisco on a riverboat. From the Barbary Coast, he could make his disappearance complete by booking immediate passage on an ocean steamer.

Kimbal allowed himself the hint of a smile. Maybe he would journey to the lovely Sandwich Islands, but if there was no departure that very same day to that paradise then he'd take passage anywhere to escape the manhunt that was sure to follow his disappearance.

Alaska. Mexico. Europe. South America. No matter. Sixteen thousand dollars was far short of the fortune that he'd anticipated, but it would be enough to live very comfortably in another country if he did not make any more foolish investments in mining stocks.

Kimbal had his over sixteen thousand dollars in less than ten minutes. He rewarded the two nervous bank employees with a smile. "You'll not forget to send the balance off to our bank in Ogden tomorrow?"

"No, sir, Mr. Kimbal." Isley shoved a brown manila envelope across the counter. "If you'll just be kind enough to sign these receipts."

Kimbal glared at the man.

"Merely a formality," Isley said, sweating nervously again.

Kimbal signed and scooped up the fat envelope of money. He shoved it into his inside coat pocket and started for the door.

When he reached it, he turned and said, "When I talk to Mr. Smithers, I will tell him that his cash shortage business need not be held against you. But we are trying to become a major bank in Nevada and it does not look good to carry such a small amount of ready cash.''

''Yes, sir!'' they both chimed as Kimbal brushed out the door.

Outside again, he headed down Virginia Street for the train station as fast as his legs would carry him. Two blocks later, Curly Cutter jumped into his path.

''Going somewhere without dividing up the big payday?'' he asked with a killing smile on his lips.

Terror flooded through the banker and his first impulse was to bolt and run. But that would be fatal. Cutter was a far younger man and he would overtake him in a moment and Kimbal could not abide the thought of being cut down from behind.

''You have twelve thousand dollars,'' Kimbal said weakly, for he had not the will to muster up his outrage. ''What in heaven's name do you want from me!''

''The rest,'' Curly said, dragging him off the sidewalk and in between two buildings, where they were immediately lost in shadows. ''I want *all* of it!''

''No!'' Kimbal cried. ''You can't do that to me! I need this money to get out of Reno and . . .''

But Curly wasn't interested. He jerked the banker up on his toes and twisted his tie until he was strangling, and then he bounced him hard against the wall, then bounced him again so that the banker's head was spinning and he was dazed.

Curly found the stuffed envelope with the sixteen thousand dollars. Kimbal tired to protest but Curly doubled up his fist and smashed him in the mouth. Kimbal tasted blood and realized he was sliding down the wall toward the ground.

''Please,'' he begged. ''If I'm caught, I'll spend my life in prison!''

Curly had started to walk away and leave him, but now,

he hesitated. "If you're caught, you'll squeal like a pig and put everyone on my trail."

"No, I swear that I won't!" Kimbal was almost sick from the terror that suddenly gripped him. Cutter was going to kill him right now!

"Yeah, you will." Curly stopped in a shaft of light and tore open the envelope. He said, "How much is in here?"

"Over sixteen thousand."

"Is that all? I had in mind a hundred thousand."

"No," Kimbal whimpered. "That's all the cash they had left today. There was never more than thirty-two thousand altogether."

"It'll have to do," Curly said. "Here's a hundred dollars and it'll buy you a train ticket to California. From there on, you are on your own. You'll think of a way to embezzle or cheat someone else out of their savings."

"A hundred dollars!" Kimbal cried. "You can't do this to me!"

"I just have." Curly laughed and it was a harsh, mocking sound. "So long, Mr. Kimbal, nice doing business with you."

He turned and headed back to the street as Kimbal drew his derringer and fired. Curly staggered, twisted around, and his Colt bucked three times at the shadows.

The banker's body jerked spasmotically in the dimness and he moaned as two of the bullets cut into his body. "Bastard," he hissed as he toppled over and lay bleeding to death. "Greedy, degenerate animal!"

CHAPTER TWENTY-ONE

Long Rider arrived in Reno shortly after midnight and immediately sought out a doctor for the woman he supported in his strong arms.

"Dr. Lawson is right down Virginia Street near the Mapes Hotel," a man who had just emerged from a saloon said. "He lives above his office and you'll have to bang the hell outta his door to wake him."

"Thanks," Gabe said, continuing along the darkened and nearly deserted street. He crossed over the Truckee River Bridge and saw the Mapes, then the doctor's office right next door.

Gabe dismounted and had to catch Hester as she slipped from his saddle. For an instant, Diablo twisted around and Gabe was caught completely defenseless with Hester cradled in his arms. "This is the chance you've been waiting for all along," Gabe said.

But the Appaloosa stallion did not strike or bite him. Instead, it turned its head and bit the horse next to it to establish its dominance. Gabe left the animal where it stood. One thing about Diablo that he was sure of was that no one was going to steal the ornery son of a bitch and ride safely away with him.

Dr. Lawson's office was lit up like Christmas and the door was unlocked, so Gabe walked in with Hester in his arms. "Doctor!"

A balding, slender man in his sixties poked his head out from a back room. "Come back later."

"I can't," Gabe said. "I got a poisoned woman for you."

"Damnation!" the doctor exclaimed with surprise. "Bring her right in and put her on my spare examining table. I tell you, when it rains it pours with misery."

Gabe brought Hester into the room, and then he stopped dead in his tracks. "Mr. Kimbal!"

"You know him?" the doctor asked as Gabe placed Hester down on the second examining table and moved quickly to the dying banker's side.

"You bet I do," Gabe said. "He's an Ogden banker."

"Well," the doctor said, sighing, "I figured he must have been a professional man. He was shot late this afternoon in an alley. Nobody can figure out why, and the man who shot him got away, though he appeared to some to have been wounded."

"But why?" Gabe touched the banker's cold cheek. "He's still alive!"

"But slipping fast," the doctor said. "He hasn't said a word since he was found. He just lies there with his eyes open, staring at my ceiling. I'd diagnose him as being brain-damaged except that he was shot in the chest instead of the head."

Gabe heaved a big sigh. "The man cheated half of Ogden out of their savings and he'd have gone to prison if he wasn't lynched first."

"Won't live to see either happen," the doctor said, turning his attention to Hester. "Poisoned, you say?"

Gabe nodded. In a few words, he explained to the doctor the tragedy he and and Polly Benton had found out near where the Truckee River seeped into the desert floor.

The doctor made a quick examination and said, "Has she been unconscious for very long?"

"No," Gabe said. "About an hour. I tried to get her here as fast as I could but I was afraid that if I galloped the pounding would kill her for certain."

"It probably would have," Dr. Lawson said. "She's in bad shape as it is. I'll try to force an emetic into her and get the woman to vomit, but I'm afraid the poison has long since gotten into her blood."

"Then how come she's still alive and her husband is dead?"

Lawson shrugged. "Maybe she drank a whole lot less of the water than her husband, and maybe her system was just stronger or more able to fight off the poison. Everybody works a little different. I don't worry about the 'why' but on the 'how' to make them recover."

"Can I try and talk to the banker?"

"Sure," Lawson said. "He's a goner anyway. You trying to recover the money or something?"

"Yeah," Gabe said as he moved over to the banker and placed his hand on the man's chest. "Mr. Kimbal, can you hear me?"

Kimbal did not react. Gabe loomed over his face and said, "Have you seen Polly? Is she all right?"

"Long Rider?" the man whispered feebly as his eyes popped open. "Is that you?"

"Yes. Is Polly all right?" Gabe was trying to fight off his own sense of rising panic. "Is she all right?"

"No," the banker breathed. "She's . . . she's with Curly Cutter. Cutter took all my money but I shot him."

Kimbal's lips twisted into the beginnings of a smile. *"I shot him!"* he repeated again, his voice growing higher and quavering.

"Where is he now?"

"I don't know," the banker said, the smile tying. "He has Polly and maybe he's killed her already."

Gabe's fingers balled up the banker's bloody shirtfront. "Damn you, Kimbal!" he raged. "You cheated a whole town and now you've maybe been the cause of a good woman's death! Why?"

Kimbal's eyelids fluttered for a moment and his breathing suddenly became strained. "I . . . I'm sorry," he gagged as his body convulsed and then suddenly went completely limp.

"Let go of him, man!" the doctor yelled, pushing Gabe aside and thumbing up Kimbal's eyelids.

"He's dead," Gabe said, heading for the door. "You better get that emetic and try and save the woman's life now. By the way, how many other doctors are there in this town?"

"Two. Dr. Potter and Dr. Crum. But I'm the best."

Just then, Hester began to cough and Gabe heard her cry, "Arthur? Arthur? Where are you?"

"Remarkable," Lawson said. "I think she's going to be all right after a long recovery."

"Just stay with her and save the poor woman's life," Gabe said as he left the office and headed down the street toward the Washoe Hotel.

He was in and out of the hotel in less than three minutes. The desk clerk had informed Gabe that Polly had not checked into the hotel and Gabe knew that she might very well be dead already. He received directions on how to find the other two doctors and headed first for Dr. Crum's house. Five minutes of banging on the physician's door finally brought the man out on his porch armed with a shotgun.

"What do you want?" Crum shouted, dressed in his pajamas.

"Did you treat a man for gunshot wounds today?"

"Hell no, but that's going to change if you don't get away from here in the next five seconds!"

Gabe left on the run. He got his directions mixed up and it took him ten extra minutes to locate Dr. Potter's house. Potter was also asleep but he was more congenial.

"What do you need?" he asked, stepping out of his house and looking at Gabe closely for signs of injury.

"I need to find a man who was shot late this afternoon. He'd be about five feet eleven inches tall. Curly hair, in his twenties. Did you treat anyone like that?"

"As a matter of fact, yes."

Gabe stepped closer. "That man is a killer and a kidnapper. I've got to find him. A woman's life is in danger."

"How do I know you're telling the truth?" Potter asked.

"You don't," Gabe said. "But if you must, then follow me over to Dr. Lawson's office. He's got the murder victim and he'll back my story."

"Then you should wake the sheriff," the doctor argued strenuously.

"Please," Gabe said. "I haven't got time for the sheriff. By the time I explained everything and he visited Lawson, took notes, and asked a bunch more questions, the kidnapper you treated could have Polly Benton twenty miles farther down the road or even have killed her."

"All right," Potter said, pulling his bathrobe around him tightly against the cold air. "The man was shot in the back and he was in real pain. But the shot wasn't fatal. I treated him, then advised him to go to bed and promised I'd come by in the morning. But he wouldn't listen. I had the feeling he was anxious to get out of town."

"By stage or train?" Gabe asked quickly.

"I don't know," Potter said. "But the only train leaving Reno is pulling out at daybreak on the way to Elko."

"Thanks," Gabe said, turning on his heel. Then he called back over his shoulder, "Where's the stagecoach line?"

"Over the river, first street go left a quarter mile. You can't miss the smell of the stable."

Gabe took off running. It seemed to him a fair assumption to make that the man he sought would go anywhere except back toward Utah. And since the wounded killer could not afford to hang around town and was in no condition to ride a horse with a bullet wound, that left only the stagecoach as his way out of Reno.

Fifteen minutes later, Gabe rode Diablo down a dark street toward the flickering lamplight of the Comstock Stage Line. The place appeared to be deserted, though Gabe figured that at least one stock tender would be sleeping on the premises.

His every nerve was tingling as he dismounted in front of the stable and then hurriedly tied Diablo to a hitching rail. The big stallion began to prance and whinny with excitement. Ignoring him, Gabe stepped up to the stage line office and pounded on the door.

"Hello in there!"

He heard a muffled cough and then a voice. "Go away. We don't open 'til six, goddamn it!"

Gabe wasn't waiting until six. He reared back and kicked the front door in and then burst into the room. It was dark but his eyes were accustomed to the dimness, and when he saw a man in heavy woolen underwear jump to his feet and reach for a shotgun, Gabe lashed out with his fist and dropped the fellow where he stood, then whirled and drew his gun, expecting more trouble.

But the man he'd punched was the only one besides

himself in the room, and now he was out cold. "Dammit," Gabe whispered.

He went back out and hurried to a water trough. Removing his Stetson, he filled it with icy water, then hurried back inside and dumped the water onto the unconscious man, who woke up spluttering and cussing.

Gabe clamped his hand over the man's mouth and shoved his head down hard on the wooden floor. "Listen to me," he said. "I'm looking for . . ."

He never finished. Curly Cutter, a prominent white bandage wound around his chest and showing between the lapels of his coat, burst in through the back of the livery office and opened fire.

Gabe dropped and drew his gun before he hit the floor. His big left hand held his six-gun but his right was fanning the hammer, and at close range the guns seemed to speak death to each other as the flames from their muzzle blasts almost touched.

Gabe had a square of white muslin for his target, and he spotted it red as Curly's gun began to lance flames upward into the ceiling. The handsome killer's feet made little mincing steps and he seemed to prance. Actually he was in a minuet of death a few seconds before he crashed over backward, half-in and half-out of the office.

"Son of a bitch!" the stage employee cried. "Don't kill me, mister. I ain't his friend!"

"The woman! Where is she?"

"In the barn. I thought . . ."

Gabe didn't hear what the man thought. He bolted over Curly's riddled body and raced across the stockyard to meet Polly, who came rolling out of a barn with her hands and feet tied and her mouth bound with a dirty gag.

Gabe untied her and removed the gag. Polly threw her arms around his neck and sobbed with relief.

"How did you find me?"

"I just looked," Long Rider said. "I just kept looking."

Polly's pretty face was bruised and her lips were puffy. Her blouse was torn open and she was covered with pieces of straw. Gabe did not need to ask if she had been badly used by Cutter in the barn. If he could have killed Curly twice, he'd have done so.

"Let's get out of here," he said.

"No, wait!" Polly said. "I have to get something first."

She walked over to Curly's body and removed a very fat and slightly bloody manila envelope from his coat pocket. Holding it up to the starlight, she said with a hint of amazement, "You put a bullet right through twenty-eight thousand dollars."

"It'll still spend," Long Rider said.

"It'll help the widow. Is Hester going to be all right?"

"The doctor made no promises, but I think so. She was awake when I left."

"Then she'll come back to Ogden with me and recover," Polly said. "And after I pay off my mortage in Salt Lake City, I'll find a way to use what money is left over to help all the others who were cheated."

"Going to take more than twenty-eight thousand dollars," Gabe said. "But I reckon that will go a long way to easing the misery that Kimbal left behind."

Polly lifted her chin and opened her arms wide for Long Rider to step into. She held him close and whispered, "That man, he's the other one that killed the Paiute woman, isn't he?"

"Yeah," Gabe said. "I'll cut off another button from his coat and make sure that Chief Spotted Horse gets it, so he knows that justice has been done."

Polly nodded and trembled, and it was several minutes before she said, "Long Rider, just make sure it's a bloody one."

At that moment, they heard wood splinter and Diablo and the tall bay mare came bursting past them. Diablo had smelled the mare and taken charge of getting her out of the corral and running free.

"There goes my rifle, and my saddle," Long Rider said as the two horses vanished in the night.

"Maybe you could catch them tomorrow after it gets light."

"Nope," Long Rider said. "They're on their way back to Utah Territory. That big stallion knows the way and there aren't horses and riders in this world fast or strong enough to catch that pair. By springtime, Diablo will have rubbed my gear away and he'll be running free."

"Maybe we'll see him again someday," Polly said quietly.

"Maybe," Long Rider conceded, "but I sure as the devil wouldn't bet the ranch on it."

WESTERNS!

at least a savings of $3.00 each month below the publishers price. Second, there is never any shipping, handling or other hidden charges—Free home delivery. What's more there is no minimum number of books you must buy, you may return any selection for full credit and you can cancel your subscription at any time. A TRUE VALUE!

Mail the coupon below

To start your subscription and receive 2 FREE WESTERNS, fill out the coupon below and mail it today. We'll send your first shipment which includes 2 FREE BOOKS as soon as we receive it.

Mail To: 557-73389
True Value Home Subscription Services, Inc.
P.O. Box 5235
120 Brighton Road
Clifton, New Jersey 07015-5235

YES! I want to start receiving the very best Westerns being published today. Send me my first shipment of 6 Westerns for me to preview FREE for 10 days. If I decide to keep them, I'll pay for just 4 of the books at the low subscriber price of $2.45 each; a total of $9.80 (a $17.70 value). Then each month I'll receive the 6 newest and best Westerns to preview Free for 10 days. If I'm not satisfied I may return them within 10 days and owe nothing. Otherwise I'll be billed at the special low subscriber rate of $2.45 each; a total of $14.70 (at least a $17.70 value) and save $3.00 off the publishers price. There are never any shipping, handling or other hidden charges. I understand I am under no obligation to purchase any number of books and I can cancel my subscription at any time, no questions asked. In any case the 2 FREE books are mine to keep.

Name _____

Address _____ Apt. # _____

City _____ State _____ Zip _____

Telephone # _____

Signature _____
(if under 18 parent or guardian must sign)
Terms and prices subject to change.
Orders subject to acceptance by True Value Home Subscription Services, Inc.